BLACK SHEEP

Skye Warren

CHAPTER ONE

I STEP INTO the dimly lit hallway, the floor-boards creaking an old, familiar sigh. Each step feels weighted, as if the house itself is trying to drag me back into the shadows of my childhood.

The air is thick, heavy with the dust of neglect and the lingering echoes of pain. I've paused on this banister so many times, the wood worn smooth by years of desperate little fingers, while I listened for my father.

Memories flood my mind, unbidden and unwelcome. The sharp crack of a hand against flesh, the muffled sobs of my mother, the metallic taste of blood in my mouth. I close my eyes, fighting back the surge of emotions that threaten to overwhelm me.

Breathe, Sienna. Just breathe.

Of course, there's no chance of him cursing or

yelling downstairs.

No chance of his fist hitting my mother's face.

He's dead now. And the man I love has been charged with his murder.

The silence is broken only by the distant ticking of a clock—a reminder of every second Logan spends sitting in jail, imprisoned because he protected me.

Which is why I can't give up.

I force myself to move, to push past the ghosts that haunt these halls. The living room looms below, a cavernous space with plastic-covered furniture. The curtains hang heavy, blocking out the sunlight, casting the room in a perpetual gloom.

Samantha said I should stay at North Security with her, but that's an hour away even in one of their fancy armored SUVs. I also could have stayed with the circus, but it's still a long bike ride away. And besides, I have too much guilt for imprisoning their leader. Where would I even sleep? In Logan's RV? No way.

My childhood home is the closest place to the jail.

It's the closest to Logan.

That's where I'll stay until he's free.

One of my old hiding places was the front

closet, my small body tucked behind the coats, my breath held tight in my lungs as I prayed for invisibility. The darkness was my sanctuary then, a place to escape the storms that raged beyond the door.

I'm not that frightened little girl anymore.

I've learned to face the darkness, to find strength in the shadows.

The circus taught me that fear is just another obstacle to overcome, that the greatest triumphs often lie on the other side of bravery.

I straighten my spine, squaring my shoulders as if preparing for battle. Which, in a way, I am. The fight for Logan's freedom won't be won in the courtroom alone—it will be fought in the hearts and minds of this town, in the whispers and the sideways glances, in the weight of prejudices that refuse to let go.

I won't let them break Logan.

I won't let them break us.

My deep breath tastes of stale air and determination, and I step into the living room, ready to face whatever lies ahead.

My mother sits at the worn dining table, a delicate teacup cradled in her hands. Banyu Cole looks small, almost fragile, as if the years of abuse have chipped away at her bit by bit, leaving only a shadow of the woman she once was.

My dad is gone, but his reign of terror hasn't stopped.

Her eyes meet mine, and for a moment, I'm struck by the weariness in her gaze, the resignation that seems to have settled into her very bones. "Hello, Sienna."

It's a look I know all too well—the face of someone who has been beaten down so many times that they've forgotten how to stand up straight.

Sympathy rushes through me. It's chased by frustration.

I want to remind her that she's stronger than this, that she doesn't have to live in the valley of my father's cruelty forever.

It's not that simple. The scars he left on her run deeper than the ones on her skin.

I bend to press a soft kiss to her cheek. "Morning, Mom."

A flicker of warmth breaking through the clouds in her eyes. "You're up early."

I nod, leaning against the doorframe to the kitchen. For some reason, I've always avoided sitting at the table, drinking tea with her. It would seem too much like defeat. "A lot on my mind."

She takes a sip of her tea, her hands trembling

slightly. "About this circus man?"

"His name's Logan, Mom." Which she knows. I run a hand through my messy hair, my thoughts spinning. "I don't know how I'm going to get him free. This isn't even about Dad, you know. It's about the fact that he protected me from Kyle. It's retribution."

My mother is quiet for a long moment, her gaze distant. "People here… They don't like outsiders. They never have."

Anger flares in my chest. "Outsiders like us?"

She sighs, setting her teacup down on the side table. "We look different."

That always upset me when I was a kid. I was born and raised in this godforsaken town, and I was always called a freak for the shape of my eyes.

I was the same as them on the inside, damn it.

At least, that's what I thought. The circus has taught me that it might not be true. There could have been a different reason they never accepted me. I wouldn't conform. I wouldn't bow to the supposed golden boy, to the town gossips. That's what made me a freak.

I glance over at my mother's cherrywood china cabinet, its rich, dark surface gleaming faintly in the muted light. It's old-fashioned, sturdy, and imposing—a testament to a time when things were built to last. It stands as sentinel against the far wall, guarding its precious contents with a solemnity that borders on reverence.

Behind the glass doors lives my mother's doll collection. Each one is a silent witness to years gone by, a testament to dreams and places far removed from Forrester's suffocating grasp. Dolls from all over the world peer out from their glass prison, their painted faces frozen in perpetual serenity.

I've always found it ironic. These delicate figurines, with their representations of beauty and culture, were trapped behind a barrier, much like my mother was between these walls.

I remember the countless times I stood before that cabinet as a child, my nose almost pressed against the glass, yearning to hold just one doll in my hands. There was an allure to them, each with its story, its secrets locked away. The one from Japan, dressed in an intricate kimono with tiny cherry blossoms embroidered on the fabric. The African doll with her vibrant dress made of kente cloth, her hair adorned with beads. A porcelain ballerina from Russia with a tutu so delicate it looked like it might dissolve at a touch.

Those dolls were forbidden treasures.

My mother's rule was absolute: look but don't

touch.

"They are not toys," she said whenever she caught me lingering too long near the cabinet. Her voice was stern, but her eyes always held a trace of something softer—a fear of what might happen if I did break one. Maybe she was scared of what breaking them would symbolize—the shattering of something beautiful that couldn't be mended.

Even now, longing pangs in my chest as I gaze at the dolls. It's mixed with defiance. They remain untouchable, perfect in their stillness, while everything around them crumbles.

"Do you still have that one from Italy?" I ask suddenly, breaking the silence.

My mother's eyes flicker toward the cabinet, and for a moment, I see a shadow of her old pride. "Yes," she says quietly. "She's right there."

I follow her gaze to a small doll dressed in traditional Italian garb—a miniature masterpiece with expressive eyes that seem almost too lifelike. She stands on her tiny stand, untouched by time or hardship.

"She's beautiful," I murmur.

"Yes," my mother echoes softly. "She is."

"How come you never open the doors? Take them out?"

She looks at me, her dark eyes shining. "They don't want to come out."

"They're just dolls," I whisper, but I know they're more than that.

"We all make our choices, Sienna. You know that better than anyone. And this circus man of yours. He knows that, too. He took the risk when he stood up to Kyle for you."

That doesn't mean I have to accept it. I've spent my whole life fighting against the unfairness of this world, and I'm not about to stop now.

Not when Logan's freedom is at stake.

I lean forward, my elbows on my knees, my eyes intense. "I have to do something. I can't just sit back and let them freaking imprison him. Kyle kidnapped me, for Christ's sake. And no one cared enough to do anything. Hell, Sheriff Dunham probably helped him."

She looks at me, and for a moment, I see a flicker of the old fire in her eyes, the spark that my father tried so hard to extinguish. "What can you possibly do?"

I take a deep breath, my mind racing. "Something. I'll figure this out. I have to."

For Logan. For us. For the life we've built together, the love we've fought so hard to build.

I won't let this town take that away from me.

No matter what it takes.

Banyu's weathered hands fidget nervously in her lap. "Perhaps it's time to… to let him go. To start a new life, away from all this. You could go anywhere, now that you don't have a man holding you down. You could leave. Start over."

A hot flash of betrayal surges through me. "How can you even say that? I would never abandon Logan, especially not now when he needs me most."

"Men always need us. That is the problem."

I push away from the doorframe and pace the worn carpet. "Have you moved on from Dad, then? Put it all behind you like it never happened? Gone to travel?"

Mom flinches, her eyes dropping to the floor. "That's different," she says quietly. "I'm old now. You're young. You still have a chance at a better life."

I whirl to face her, my voice rising with passion. "A better life? Mom, you can have a better life too, at any age! Look at these curtains." I gesture to the heavy drapes, blocking out the sunlight. "They're like prison bars. They're still there because you keep them there."

"I deserve them," she whispers, her voice thick with unshed tears.

My heart clenches. I kneel before her, taking her hands in mine. "No. No one deserves this." I squeeze her fingers, willing her to believe me. "It's not too late. You can tear down these curtains, let the light in. You can still find happiness."

She meets my gaze, her dark eyes so like my own, filled with a lifetime of pain and fear. "I don't know if I'm strong enough," she admits, her voice barely audible. "I've never been like you."

I smile softly, brushing a stray curl from her forehead. "You are, Mom. You're strong and loyal. Where do you think I got it from?" I stand, pulling her to her feet with me. "I'll prove that to you, somehow. First, I need to save Logan."

A tentative smile touched her lips. "If anyone can do it, you can."

I release her hands, my resolve solidifying like steel in my veins.

The hold of Forrester goes deeper than my father's fists ever did. It's about legacy, about prejudice so ingrained it's like a stain on the very fabric of the land.

My phone buzzes with an incoming text.

On my way. That's Maisie. The corner of my lips tugs upwards.

She's one of the only people who stood by my side all these years, even though she's part of the town. The sweetheart. Voted most friendly. If anyone can get through to them, she can.

I run upstairs to take a quick shower. The hot water ends in about ninety seconds in this house, so I hurry through the shampoo. The thought of confronting my past, of facing the whispers and the stares, makes my stomach churn. I've spent so long running from it all, finding solace in the circus. Now I have to run toward it. I have to face it head-on.

A shiver takes me as I step out of the shower. Even in the oppressive heat, it's always cold in the moments of tepid water and peeling linoleum of my bathroom.

I stare at myself in the mirror, this face I used to hate, with its too-large eyes and nose and lips. With its big foreign features. *Freak. Whore. Outsider.* I'm Sienna Mae Cole. I've survived worse than small-town gossip. I've survived my father's fists, my mother's tears, Kyle's cruelty.

There's a silver lining, after all. It means I have enough strength to save Logan.

When I get back downstairs, I'm surprised to find a mug of coffee waiting for me.

My mom hates coffee. She only made it for my father, who would hit her if it wasn't ready and hot whenever he wanted it, which naturally made her hate the smell even more. I prefer coffee to tea, but she never makes it for me. I would never ask.

Except today she's holding a steaming mug for me. The liquid is already pale from cream and sugar. "Mom. You didn't have to do this."

"I wanted to."

"I'm going to fight for him. But more than that, I'm going to fight for us. For the support we never got but should have. And I'm going to win because I have something they don't."

She tilts her head, curiosity brightening her dark eyes. "What's that?"

I take a big gulp of coffee, burning my lips, my tongue. It's never felt better. "Good old-fashioned stubbornness. I got that from you, too."

Banyu laughs softly, and for a moment, I see a glimmer of the woman she used to be before my father's abuse snuffed out her light. "Yes. You are my daughter."

Tears prick my eyes, but I turn to slip on my shoes from the mat by the door. I pause, looking back at her. "Love you. I'll be back soon."

She smiles, and it's like the sun peeking through storm clouds. "Be careful."

I wink at her, my hand on the doorknob. "Careful? Where's the fun in that?"

And with a laugh, I step out into the waiting day, ready to face whatever comes my way. For Logan. For us. For the family I found under the big top.

The sound of tires crunching over gravel pulls my attention to the street. Maisie's car, a cheerful yellow VW bug that seems out of place in this neighborhood of faded dreams, rolls to a stop by the curb. She waves at me through the window, her smile bright, her curls reflecting the sun.

I hurry down the steps, my boots thudding against the worn wood. As I approach the car, Maisie leans over to push open the passenger door.

Tricks comes bounding out, his little legs moving faster than they should be able to. His ears—one up, one flopped down—flap as he sprints toward me. I drop to my knees, arms wide open.

"Tricks!" My voice catches in my throat.

He leaps into my arms, wriggling with joy. His tiny body trembles with excitement, and I bury my face in his fur. It's softer than I remember, and it smells faintly of Maisie's lavender shampoo. Tears prick my eyes, but I blink them away quickly. I don't want Maisie to see me cry.

"You missed me, huh?" I whisper against

Tricks's warm fur. He licks my cheek enthusiastically, his tail wagging so hard it's a blur.

Maisie steps out of the car, a knowing smile on her lips. "Hey there, stranger," she says. "Ready for a jailbreak?"

Tricks wiggles in my arms and barks softly as if agreeing with Maisie.

I slide into the seat, the leather cool against my skin. "I wish."

When we're all buckled in, Maisie pulls away from the curb, the car lurching forward with a burst of speed. She glances over at me, her brow furrowed. "You okay? For real?"

Anyone could see the dark shadows beneath my eyes. I shrug, turning to stare out the window at the passing houses, their façades as familiar as old scars. "I'm fine," I lie. "This is just my face."

Maisie snorts, the sound inelegant and utterly her. "Bullshit," she says, her tone blunt. "I know you. You're not going to sleep until he's free again."

I sigh, my shoulders slumping. It feels good to cuddle Tricks as I think about this. "Of course I'm not," I admit, my voice raw. "They've got him locked up like some kind of animal. Like he's a danger to society. Meanwhile Kyle is walking free for what he did to me."

Maisie reaches over, her hand finding mine and squeezing gently. "We're going to get him out," she says, her words fierce with conviction. "We're going to prove his innocence."

I nod, swallowing past the lump in my throat.

She doesn't know the truth.

That Logan isn't actually innocent. He did beat my father, but he did it to protect me. The law in this part of the country, these rural backwoods, has no place for nuance. No mercy for outsiders, even if he killed a man who beat my mother every night.

"How's he been?" I ask, forcing lightness into my tone.

She glances sideways at Tricks, who's still wriggling in my lap. "He's been a very good boy. Haven't you, Tricks? And he's taken a shine to our girls. He keeps cleaning Camila's ears."

"Aww. Is that true, Tricks? Do you have a little crush?" My mother refuses to have pets in the house. Even a small, friendly one like Tricks. Which means he's staying with Maisie until I'm out of here.

"And he *really* likes June Bug. He's tried humping her a few times."

"Oh shit. I guess I need to get him fixed. I didn't even think of that."

Maisie laughs. "Don't worry. June Bug had no problem laying down some boundaries. Plus she's fixed. So we're not going to end up with a bunch of puppies. Even though they would be adorable. I'd have content for months."

Content. I blink as we turn into the town proper, an idea nudging me. She takes videos of her two dogs' antics that go viral online. The platforms pay her for the views. Plus she gets dog toys and fancy human-grade dog food sent to them for free. There's the occasional sponsored post. It's not a ton of money, but it's more than I made working at the coffee shop when I still lived here.

I turn back to the window, watching the houses give way to fields of withered crops, the land as barren and unforgiving as the people who inhabit it.

"Hey," I say. "About that content."

"Yeahhh?" she asks, her voice drawn out.

"What if you made videos on behalf of Logan? Told his story?"

"Okay, but why?"

"I don't know." Except I do. The town's prejudice runs deep, as thick and choking as the dust that coats everything here. Even Maisie, with her sunny optimism and unwavering loyalty, can't entirely escape its grasp. "Maybe we can convince the town, sway them. Or even if we can't, maybe we can convince the world."

"Convincing the world would be easier."

"They don't have any proof. It could put pressure on them."

The county jail looms ahead, a squat, ugly building that seems to leach the color from the world around it. Maisie pulls into the parking lot, the car shuddering to a stop.

"It's worth a shot," she says, her hand on the door handle. "Consider me hired."

I take a deep breath, squaring my shoulders. "Thank you, Maisie. Really. I—"

"Oh, shut up," she says. "Don't get all mushy on me now. I just promised to make a few videos that probably won't do anything. Besides, I'm your best friend."

My best friend. Tears prick my eyes, but I try not to get mushy.

We step out into the harsh sunlight, the heat pressing down like a physical weight. I focus on the rush of my blood, the unshakable certainty that I will prevail. That I have to, because the town would just as soon watch me burn.

CHAPTER TWO

THE COUNTY JAIL smells of desperation.

And stale coffee.

My heart pounds as I scan the grim, unfriendly faces who fill the pens on the other side of the reception desk. Cops who have picked up my father countless times for violent behavior.

Cops who then released him back to our house.

They didn't care about him then.

And they wouldn't care now, if not for Kyle and his influential family.

I long for Logan's familiar chiseled features. Worry churns in my gut seeing him in a place like this, caged and alone, surrounded by people who don't give a shit.

The receptionist gives me a glare when I give her my name, but she reluctantly calls someone in the back. I expect some low-level deputy. Instead it's the sheriff himself who comes.

I can tell why he wanted to see me.

He doesn't even bother to hide his smugness.

"Well, if it isn't Sienna Mae Cole," he drawls, his tone dripping with derision. "I thought the town got rid of you. Guess you came back. Like a tick you can't get rid of."

As if he doesn't know exactly whose trunk I came in on.

"Spare me the bullshit." My pulse races, but I won't give him the satisfaction of seeing me crumble. "I'm here to see Logan Whitmere. And you can't legally stop me."

He steps closer, the smell of tobacco and cheap aftershave making my stomach churn. "You know, it's only a matter of time before he's convicted. Should start thinking about moving on. I might be willing to overlook that loose pussy of yours and give you a ride."

I clench my fists, nails digging into my palms. "You will never touch me."

"Oh? You're so sure about that?" He leans in, his breath hot against my ear. "I bet you learned some wild moves out there in the circus. Always took after your mother, didn't you?"

I manage not to flinch. This is an old wound.

"You wish you knew."

His laugh is a cold, sharp sound that cuts through me. "I know I know all about you and the Cole family. Hard to forget. This town don't forget, matter of fact. And it certainly doesn't forgive."

"Fuck you." My voice shakes despite my efforts.

He straightens and adjusts his belt, lips twisted in contemptuous amusement. "The evidence is stacking up against him. You won't be proud much longer."

I glare at him, every muscle in my body taut with anger and frustration. "You're enjoying this, aren't you? Watching people suffer."

His smirk widens. "People like you and Logan? Yeah, it's kinda satisfying seeing the freaks of the world get what's coming."

"You're the freak."

"And you're the town slut." He turns away from me with a dismissive wave of his hand. "Fucking around with the circus didn't change that none. Enjoy your visit while you can."

He nods toward a young man in uniform who hurries over to escort me back. My heart pounds in my chest as I turn away from the sheriff, which feels like turning away from a wild animal who's starving. As if I might get a bite taken out of me.

Town slut.

That's what they call me here. As if that means anything. As if a single one of them ever got me into bed with them. They wish. They wish and wish so hard it turns into violence. I don't know how that works exactly, what dark alchemy they use, but God is it effective.

The deputy leads me back, past the bullpen, past the offices.

Toward the single jail cell.

I've taken this walk before, though it's been a long time.

My mother used to come and bail out my father. I trailed after her as a five-year-old. My father would stumble out of the backroom jail cells, stinking of liquor and piss.

Then when I got older, they stopped doing the whole bail thing.

We couldn't afford it anymore, and they didn't want to keep him any more than we wanted to bring him home. So they started letting him walk it off on his way home.

The deputy unlocks the heavy metal door leading to the county's singular jail cell. A clang of solid metal door echoes through the small space, and I step inside, fighting to keep my composure.

The cell comes into view—metal bars stark against the dim light—and there he is: Logan, looking more weary than I've ever seen him.

His tall frame leans back on a metal stool, shoulders bowed under the weight of his new reality, eyes closed. He doesn't even look up, though he must have heard the door open.

"Logan..." My voice is barely above a whisper.

His gaze snaps to me, dark hazel eyes sharp despite his posture. Even rumpled and unshaven, his raw masculine beauty steals my breath.

He stands slowly, moving closer to the bars. "Sunset."

I rush forward, almost tripping in my haste to reach him.

My chest tightens at the familiar nickname. "Are you okay?"

His fingers twitch like he wants to touch me, but he drops his hands. Purple shadows underscore his eyes. "I'm fine. This isn't my first night in a place like this. Won't be the last."

I put my hand toward the bars, reaching through them.

The officer clears his throat. "You can't touch them, miss. For safety reasons."

My eyes narrow. "He isn't going to hurt me."

The officer looks a little sheepish but also resolute. "It's protocol."

Protocol. I long to tell him how much pain and suffering their protocol caused my mother through the years. Doesn't matter, though.

I unclench my hands from the metal bars and take a step back.

"Hey," Logan says, pulling my attention back. "Don't worry."

"Don't worry?" A brittle laugh. "You're locked up like an animal. Kyle should be the one inside there, if anything. Of course I'm going to worry."

A ghost of a smile flickers across his lips. "I'll be out of here in no time."

The words ring false. I shake my head, dark hair falling in my face. He's always trying to protect me, even now. But I see the cracks in his calm façade, the tension coiled in his broad shoulders. The shadows that linger in his beautiful green eyes.

I lower my voice. "Listen to me. I'm going to figure this out."

His Adam's apple bobs as he swallows hard, stormy eyes holding mine. For a heartbeat, his walls crumble and I glimpse the lost, broken boy within the hardened man, the one who's struggling the most inside this cage.

Then he blinks, and it's gone, replaced by determination.

"You shouldn't even be here," he says.

"Of course I should." First my mother and now him. As if I could be inconstant. As if there's even a choice. "Would you leave me in jail alone if it were reversed?"

He shakes his head, swearing. "It isn't the same."

"You're right. It's worse."

He takes a deep breath, but it doesn't work. The storm inside him rages just beneath the surface. "The circus's lawyer is already on this. He's good—one of the best in the country. Landed this morning. He's already working on my defense."

I want to trust that, but seeing him here, locked up like an animal, it's hard to hold on to that hope. "Logan—" I start, but he cuts me off with a hard look.

"You need to get out of here. You've got enough on your plate without worrying about me. Go back to the circus, take care of Tricks, and everything will be fine."

Frustration makes my throat tighten. "Logan."

"Don't visit me again."

His words sting, even though I know he means well. He always tries to protect me, but this time it feels like he's pushing me away. "You really think I can just go back and pretend?"

"Yes," he says, his gaze locking on to mine with an intensity that makes my heart ache. "I need you to be strong. If that means pretending you never met me, then so be it."

I swallow hard, fighting back tears. "You're losing hope."

"The lawyer will handle this," he says, a hint of desperation seeping into his words despite his calm façade. "And I'm fine in here. I've been through worse."

"That's not exactly a ringing endorsement of the accommodations."

"Promise me," he says, eyes boring into mine. "Promise you won't come back here."

Why the hell is he pushing this? Does he think I'm going to judge him for the scruff on his jaw or the rumpled state of his clothes? Does he think I'm going to look down on him for protecting me? That's when I realize it's about more than that.

Those things are surface level.

This goes far deeper.

"Please," he adds softly.

"You're not your father."

A muscle pulsing in his jaw. "This isn't about him," he mutters.

I reach through the bars as far as I can, my fingertips brushing against the cold metal, ignoring the deputy who thankfully has started looking at his phone. "Isn't it? He was locked up. By bars, by prejudice. By his shame. This must feel like the same thing."

Logan's gaze hardens. "You don't know what you're talking about."

"You're a better man than he ever was. He was a victim of his circumstance."

"And what am I?" he says, the bitterness in his voice like a slap. "The ringmaster of the toilet bowl? The owner of the cot? The valiant champion of the fucking jail cell?"

"You're a fighter. So fight this." *Please.*

He steps back, breaking our tenuous connection through the bars. "It's not that simple."

"Then make it simple." I'm not above pleading. "You've spent your life running from his shadow, but you've never been him. You're not a monster."

He runs a hand through his tousled hair. "I know that."

I grip the bars tighter, desperation clawing at me from the inside out. "Do you? Because right now, it feels like you're giving up."

Logan's shoulders slump slightly, the fight seeming to drain out of him. "I'm not giving up. I'm trying to protect you."

My heart aches. "And look what that got you?"

His gaze sharpens. "This wasn't your fault."

"I'm not going to promise that I won't come back, because I am. Again and again, until you're out of there. Whatever it takes. But you're going to make me a promise." I blink back tears. "Promise me you won't let this place break you. Promise me you'll fight."

The hard emerald gaze holds mine.

An endless heartbeat of *no, I can't, it's already happening.*

Neither of us will get the promises we want today.

The young officer clears his throat.

Reluctantly, I step back. "I'll come back soon."

Logan gives a short shake of his head, his jaw clenched tight, a muscle twitching beneath the surface. Don't come, it says. To hell with that, my raised eyebrow says in return.

I follow the young officer back to the reception area, shoulders slumped, feet heavy. The sheriff's smug face catches my eye. He stands triumphantly, arms crossed, a smirk playing on his thin lips. The bastard thinks he's already won, that Logan's fate is sealed.

Rage simmers beneath my skin.

The stale air clings to my skin, the weight of this place threatening to suffocate me. I quicken my pace, desperate to escape the oppressive walls. Bursting through the exit, I gulp in the fresh air, my lungs expanding with a shuddering breath.

The sun's rays burn too bright, too cheerful for the shadows inside me.

Maisie stands on the curb, holding Tricks.

My eyebrows rise when I see who's joined her.

Wolfgang's black jeans and a black T-shirt hug a thickly muscled body. His sharp gaze is responsible for the elaborate, scary-accurate knife throws that entertain Cirque des Miroirs' audience. He has an air of expecting trouble, as if he's ready for anything.

"Hi, Wolfgang. I was just going to come look for you."

"I'm here to take you back home," he says in his gravelly voice.

Maisie frowns. "I told him I'm the one bringing you home."

"And I told you to leave," Wolfgang says to her, his tone curt. Very curt.

Despite his imposing size, he's usually nicer than that.

And Maisie has lost her usual aplomb.

Her pretty face flushes pink. "And I told *you* not to interfere."

"Logan asked me to keep an eye on Sienna. And her nosy little friend."

Maisie's mouth drops open, but she doesn't seem particularly pissed at the man inside the jail. It's more like she's mad at Wolfgang. And it doesn't sound like something Logan would say. No, it seems like Wolfgang just said that to goad her.

His tall frame looms over her, but she doesn't back down.

"Nosy?" she says. "The only nosy thing here is you trying to boss me around."

If I didn't know better, I would think it was flirting.

I glance back at the imposing building one last time, determination burning in my chest. I will do whatever it takes to bring him back where he belongs—with me.

I turn back to my friends from different

worlds. "I'm not going back home. I need to speak with the lawyer who's working on Logan's defense."

Wolfgang's expression softens slightly, which isn't saying much. "He wants to ask you some questions, but he can come to your mother's house."

"I'd rather go to him. Where is he? With the circus?"

"Yes. I suppose I could take you, but you shouldn't come to the jail again. I can pass on any messages. It's not safe for you here. I don't trust that sheriff."

"To hell with that."

Maisie rolls her eyes. "See? Nosy. Controlling. Bossy."

I can't help a small laugh at my friend. "Maisie."

She huffs. "Fine, but you don't need babysitting. And neither do I."

Wolfgang narrows his eyes at my best friend. "No? You're about as tall as a toddler. And having a little tantrum, too. So I'd say you could use all the protection you can get."

Oh dear. Maisie's blue eyes spark with venom.

This is going to get ugly.

Or it would, if I had time to enjoy the show.

"Maisie," I say, catching her before she explodes in what would undoubtedly be the most adorable tirade in history. "I really need to talk to this lawyer. You can destroy Wolfgang later, okay?"

CHAPTER THREE

WOLFGANG'S PICKUP TRUCK rumbles down the dusty road, the familiar scent of leather and metal filling the cab. I rest my head against the window, the vibration humming through my skull as I watch the green hills blur by. Forrester's buildings shrink in the rearview mirror, replaced by sprawling fields and distant woods.

We pull out onto the country road. Doubts wrap like dark tendrils around my heart.

"Is the circus open for business?" I ask, breaking the silence.

He snorts, a sound filled with derision. "Nah, they're taking a break."

"They must be going stir crazy," I say, knowing they love the rapid pace.

The hard lines of his face are set in a grim expression. "Hardly likely to perform for the assholes who locked us up."

"The sheriff?"

"The entire rinky-dink city that was too small for us in the first place. They don't trust us," he continues, eyes never leaving the road. "And we don't trust them."

The weight of his words settles in my chest.

The townspeople have always eyed the circus with suspicion, but now it's worse. It's like they're waiting for them to slip up, to confirm their worst fears.

The term *powder keg* seems to apply.

I swallow around a knot. "I'm sorry."

"Not your fault."

"I'm supposed to believe everyone agrees with you?"

He sighs. "They're worried. We've faced a lot of shit in our day, but this is a new one."

"We'll figure it out."

"Logan will. He always done."

I offer a weak smile in return. "Right."

We fall into silence, the only sounds are the engine's growl and the crunch of gravel beneath the tires. My thoughts drift to Logan, locked away in that cell. The haunted look in his eyes lingers in my mind. He's figured out plenty, built an entire community in the circus, but I'm not sure if he's capable of doing it now.

The pickup truck continues its steady journey, each mile taking us farther from Forrester, farther from Logan. And deeper toward people who blame me for their problems.

"So, who is this lawyer? Did you guys check his references?"

A grunt. "We didn't just hire him. He's been working for the circus for years. Flies out whenever we need something. He's real good."

"Get murder charges often?"

"We get into enough trouble to test him." He glances at me briefly before returning his focus to the road. "If anyone can save Logan, it's him."

"But it might not be enough," I fill in, my voice flat. "Logan needs to get out of there. Sooner rather than later. The jail is wearing on him."

"Because of his father."

It's not a question. "You know about that?"

"The surprise is that you do."

"I can't believe he'd think he was like him. Logan would never hurt anyone."

A gruff throat clearing. "Well, that's not strictly true."

He did hurt my father. And Kyle. They deserved it. "He'd never hurt a woman, which is what his father did."

Wolfgang tightens his grip on the wheel. "The past has its claws in all of us. Some people may think they're free. That's just an illusion. We never really get to move on."

"Bullshit," I say, frustration bubbling up inside me.

"Prove me wrong," he replies, his voice tinged with a rare softness.

I can't, because the past has its claws in me as deep as ever. Seems like he already knew that. I don't enjoy being transparent. I turn back to the window, watching the landscape blur by. The silence between us is heavy, filled with unspoken doubts and what-ifs.

"Logan wouldn't want you worrying like this," he says.

"He doesn't get a say right now," I snap back, harsher than I intended.

A nod. "But going off half-cocked won't help him."

"I'm not going to sit on my ass and do nothing."

Wolfgang's lips twitch, the barest hint of a smile. "Stubborn as a mule, you are. No wonder he loves you."

My heart stutters in my chest. *Love.*

The word hangs in the air between us, heavy with unspoken implications. I swallow hard, forcing myself to gaze out the window at the barren fields flying by. He told me he loved me. That was before. Now he doesn't even want me to visit him. "What if he doesn't love me?"

"He isn't in jail right now because you're a good lay."

"Funny. That's the only thing the town thinks I'm good for."

"You love him back. Don't bother denying it."

Wasn't going to. "He protects people. It's what he does. Women, especially. Look at Alessandra. He took over the freaking circus for her."

"He was young and hopeful and idealistic. The circus isn't an easy life. It tends to crush people like him, but he turned it around. But he never loved her. I've known him for years and never seen him this gone over a woman."

My throat feels thick. "All the more reason I need to fix this."

"Told you. He's going to fix it himself."

The pickup truck rumbles into the old Hendrick's farm. A once-vibrant Cirque des Miroirs camp feels eerily subdued. Every flag is furled, hanging limply against their poles. The usual cacophony of laughter, music, and shouts is absent. Instead, a heavy silence blankets everything.

Wolfgang pulls into the makeshift parking area and kills the engine. The sudden quiet is almost deafening after the constant rumble of the truck.

"Let's get inside," he says, stepping out and waiting for me to follow.

I walk through the grounds, my footsteps crunching on the sun-burned grass.

"Everyone's on edge," Wolfgang mutters, more to himself than to me.

It's mostly deserted with the rare worker or performer moving with downcast eyes and hushed whispers, their faces etched with worry. A few glance at me with narrowed eyes. They're suspicious of me. Maybe they're right to be.

Wolfgang stops in front of the massive, modern RV that I recognize as the main operations center. Apparently it's also serving as the command center for Logan's defense. Its sleek exterior feels out of place among the vintage charm of the circus.

Before I can climb the metal steps, an elegant figure blocks my path.

The ringmaster stands there with his arms crossed and a dark eyebrow raised. His custom-tailored suit is as impeccable as ever, a sharp contrast to Wolfgang's rough-edged masculinity. Pure hostility darkens his handsome face.

"Well, well," Emerson drawls. "Look who decided to grace us with her presence. Quite the surprise, considering you're the one who landed us in this mess."

"Move aside," I say stonily.

"Oh, I think you've done more than enough. Your little spat with Kyle—your friendly neighborhood sociopath—set off this chain of events."

"Getting kidnapped isn't exactly a spat. I didn't ask for any of his."

"True." His gaze takes in my body from head to toe with insolent slowness. "I suppose your charms are just too irresistible to the rustic menfolk of this town."

His derisive tone makes it clear what he thinks of my supposed charms.

My hands tighten into fists. "I'm going inside."

Wolfgang steps toward his friend. "This isn't helping."

Emerson holds up his hands in mock surrender. "Et tu, Wolfgang?"

"Save your commentary for later," Wolfgang growls. "For when Logan is out of jail and he can punch you in the face for it."

I glare at Emerson. "I didn't ask for any of this, but unlike some people, I'm not going to sit around and make snarky comments about it. I'm going to actually fix it."

Emerson gives a charming smile, one that makes chills run down my spine. "Oh, I'm well aware of your penchant for action, darling. It's just that your actions often lead us into delightful little predicaments."

"You're wasting your time, and what's worse, you're wasting Logan's."

"She's right," Wolfgang says. "Let her give her statement."

Emerson rolls his eyes. "Fine, fine. Go ahead and tell them about how Patrick Cole beat Logan's girlfriend. Nothing like a little motive to tighten up a case."

Shit. "They also show a pattern of violent behavior. My dad got into fights with everyone. Which means everyone in town has motive."

Emerson tilts his head, considering me. "You've got spirit. I'll give you that." He leans closer, his voice dropping to a conspiratorial whisper. "Though I can't *quite* recall. Where did you get your law degree from?"

Wolfgang grunts. "Fuck off, Em. I'm serious."

"Ah, I see Logan has assigned his guard dog to the task of protecting her." He straightens up and gestures grandly toward the RV's door. "After you, then, Miss Cole. I'm eager to watch you save the day. The fate of the circus is apparently in your hands."

CHAPTER FOUR

"THAT'S WHEN THE sheriff arrested Logan right there by the bonfire."

The words taste like sawdust in my mouth. My voice has grown hoarse by the time I finish recounting the events of that night. My heart weighs a thousand pounds.

Harrison finishes taking notes with a scratch of his pen. "Thank you, Miss Cole."

He clicks off a recording device.

"Please. I have to know about your plans. About getting him out."

He leans back in his chair, loosening his tie with a sigh. "I'm afraid I have some difficult news. The evidence… It doesn't look good for Logan."

My stomach clenches. "What evidence? If someone says they saw something, they're lying. This whole town is corrupt. It's revenge for him beating up Kyle."

Harrison meets my gaze, his eyes kind but grim. "They have a metal crowbar from the scene. It has Logan's fingerprints on it. And… it has traces of your stepfather's blood."

My mouth drops open. "What?"

"The forensics are damning."

"When did they find this? Because the supposed crime happened a long time ago. Outdoors. How could fingerprints and DNA have lasted that long?"

"According to the prosecutor, it was found by the EMS who took him to the hospital. They have documentation showing it was checked into evidence, though they didn't run the DNA until last week, after he was arrested. And fingerprinted."

Holy shit. "In other words, the entire thing is a frame job. I don't suppose the evidence room is run by anything with actual timestamps or anything."

"It's all slips of paper, like we're in the dark ages." Harrison rubs his temples, looking grim under the harsh lights of the modern RV. "Unfortunately, I'm familiar with the way some of these small towns operate. It's part of why they keep me on retainer. Though they're not usually facing murder charges."

Memories flash through my mind—his strong, safe arms around me; the tender brush of his calloused hands; the fierce protectiveness in his eyes whenever someone threatened me or the circus.

I slump back in my chair, an icy numbness spreading through my veins. This can't be happening. Logan's fingerprints, Patrick's blood—it's bad.

"You're going to get him out, aren't you?" I manage to choke out, my voice sounding small and lost even to my own ears.

"I'm going to try." Harrison's mouth presses into a hard line. "But this new 'evidence' changes things. We won't be able to get a quick dismissal the way I'd hoped. It won't be quick at all, considering the county prosecutor is still out of town."

"I'm working on that."

His eyebrows rise. "Good. No, don't tell me how. We have an extremely difficult case ahead of us, and I'll take all the help I can get. We're heading in to a jury trial."

"That's total bullshit. Literally no one in the county can be impartial about this."

"Jury selection will just be one of the hurdles

we face. The physical evidence ties Logan directly to the attack. Coupled with his romantic history with you, as well as your father's documented physical abuse, the prosecution will argue motive and opportunity."

I swallow hard against the bile rising in my throat. This is a nightmare. "It's fucked up that no one cared about my father's 'documented physical abuse' until they wanted to hurt us."

Us. We're an us now. Logan is my anchor in a chaotic world, the only family I've ever truly known. The thought of losing him, of him going away forever… It's unbearable.

But how can we fight physical freaking evidence?

My mind spins with desperate possibilities, each more futile than the last. It's one thing to fight a prejudiced system, but corruption that goes this far?

They can invent any kind of evidence they want.

He meets my gaze solemnly, the weight of the world in his eyes. "Unfortunately, there's more bad news. A source I have in the sheriff's office informed me they'll be going for murder one. Premeditated."

Holy shit. "That means… the death penalty?"

"It wouldn't be a foregone conclusion. But it would be possible."

"That can't happen. I mean, that *can't* happen. What do we do?"

"We gather information. They've had far longer to prep their case."

"And a willingness to make up whatever they want."

"Perhaps, but we can't do that. So we need to find actual evidence. I'm questioning everyone. As you can imagine, I'm hitting more than one brick wall."

As the gravity of the situation crashes over me, hot tears sting my eyes. I blink them back, squaring my shoulders. I won't give up. Even if it means going to war with this whole damn town.

"Subpoenas will be a tool we'll use in trial," he says. "But by then witnesses might be tampered with. Actual physical evidence might be destroyed, assuming there ever was any."

Wolfgang snorts, having leaned back in his chair from across the RV. "As if Logan would ever be so careless as to leave physical evidence. It's insulting."

"Yes," Emerson says, his tone ironic. "That's what we should tell the judge. Logan would never be so careless as to leave a crowbar behind when he beats someone to death."

"He wouldn't even use a crowbar," Wolfgang says, sounding offended. "He uses his fists like a goddamn man. Is it his fault that the other man is too damned drunk to defend himself?"

"According to the law, yes," Harrison says.

Tears prick my eyes. "My father could have accidentally killed a hundred people. He's gotten into a million drunken bar fights."

"Well, he wasn't very good at them," Emerson says, sounding droll. "A shame when a man is penalized for being competent."

Wolfgang curses. "That damned sheriff needs to be called out."

Harrison holds up a placating hand. "Accusing him without proof will not help. It could even make things worse."

"Well then, we'll just have to find some proof, won't we?" Emerson drawls from his perch on the couch, examining his fingernails with an air of nonchalance. "Perhaps our resident knife thrower can procure one of the sheriff's crowbars for comparison."

Wolfgang glowers at him, but I can see the wheels turning behind his icy blue eyes.

Harrison clears his throat. "I would advise against any illegal actions. The best thing we can do right now is build a strong defense. Character witnesses, alibi statements, poking holes in the prosecution's case. We need to focus on winning. And not actually implying that Logan did anything, with or without a crowbar, ideally."

Cat bursts into the room, her small elfin face flushed, curly hair wild. She's the daughter of Alessandra, the not-so-nice fortune teller who helped Kyle kidnap me. "Guys, we've got a situation. Felix and Rocco are about to tear each other apart."

Wolfgang is on his feet in an instant, coiled and ready for a fight. Even when he's out the door, Emerson lounges on the couch.

"What, you're not going?" Cat demands. "He'll need help."

He waves a dismissive hand. "And risk this handsome face catching a stray fist? No, thank you. I'm sure Wolfgang has it under control. With his fists. No crowbars for that one."

"This isn't a joke!" I snap, my patience splintering. "Logan is locked up, the circus is falling apart, and you're just—just sitting there, being useless!"

He regards me for a long moment, his gaze pondering.

Cat and I both glare at him until he sighs,

making a great show of standing, straightening his white dress shirt and black slacks. "I suppose I can bestow some of my managerial wisdom on our fractious friends."

He saunters toward the door, pausing to glance back at me over his shoulder. His voice is mocking. "Chin up, buttercups. We'll weather this storm, like we always do. The show must go on and all that."

He disappears, I drop my head into my hands, my chest aching.

A sigh racks Cat's small frame.

She and I have never been close, but I'm worried about her expression.

I glance over at Cat, who's nervously biting her lip. Her eyes dart around the RV, like she's searching for the right words. Tension crackles in the air, thicker than ever. "What's wrong?"

She hesitates, her fingers twisting a strand of hair. "Without Logan, the circus is coming apart at the seams."

"What do you mean?" I sit up straighter, my pulse quickening.

"Some of the performers want to keep touring without him. They think we should just… move on." Her voice trembles slightly. "Like continue with the tour schedule that we had before he brought us back here and got arrested."

"What the hell?"

"Others are talking about breaking into the county jail to free him."

"They can't be serious."

She looks at me with wide eyes, pleading for me to understand. "Everyone's scared, Sienna. They don't know what to do without Logan."

Panic bubbles up inside me. "If they try to break him out, it'll be a disaster. We'll be turning this town against us even more. An all-out war between the circus and Forrester is the last thing we need."

Cat pales. "I know. But they're desperate. They don't trust the legal system here, and honestly… can you blame them?"

"No, but…" We're already in deep enough trouble as it is. We don't need vigilante justice making things worse. "Who's leading this insanity?"

"Felix is the most vocal," Cat says. "That's what he was fighting with Rocco about."

"People are going to get hurt like that."

Cat steps closer, her voice lowering to a whisper. "It's not just chaos from inside the circus. One of our best performers got an offer from a recruiter from a competing circus."

My heart skips a beat. "Who?"

"Nadia," Cat says, her eyes wide with worry. "You know how good she is. Without Logan, people are scared we won't make it. That the circus won't survive."

Nadia Perchenko is the best aerial performer here, her performances breathtaking and magnetic. She's a world-class gymnast who was courted by circuses when she went private. If she leaves, it will be a huge blow to both Cirque des Miroirs and to Logan.

"But Logan treats everyone so well," I murmur, more to myself than to Cat. "Will they get that somewhere else?"

"No, but they're worried he won't get released," Cat explains, her frustration evident. "Our performers are the best. The other circuses know this. Now that he's locked up, they think they can swoop in and steal our talent."

Desperation claws at my insides. "Is there any way we can... pay them something? To make them stay? Like some kind of bonus to help tide them over?"

Cat blinks at me, surprise flickering across her face. "Oh no, we're all getting full pay. That's one of the huge perks of working here."

My brow furrows in confusion. "Full pay?

Even when you're not performing?"

"Yeah." Cat nods emphatically. "When other circuses get rained out or stalled in traffic or anything that causes them to miss a show, they usually get no money. But not here. They call it a hazard delay, and we get our full paychecks. So this, Logan being in jail, counts."

Hazard delay.

Yes, this certainly qualifies.

"Why would they even consider leaving if they're still getting paid?" My voice cracks, the frustration evident.

Cat's eyes soften with a mixture of pity and understanding. "Because the circus isn't just a job for them. It's their life. They need to perform. It's in their blood. Asking them to sit around, even if they're getting paid, is like asking a fish not to swim."

I knew the performers were passionate about their craft, but I hadn't realized just how deep that connection runs. It makes sense, unfortunately. They thrive on the adrenaline, the applause, the sense of purpose that comes with every act.

My mind races, a whirlwind of panic and helplessness. The thought of performers leaving while Logan is in jail twists my stomach into knots. That's all he needs on top of a murder charge—his circus falling apart because people can't stand waiting around.

I straighten my spine. "Where are they?"

She blinks, caught off guard by my sudden resolve. "Some of them are in the main tent, discussing things."

I burst out of the RV and take off toward the main tent, my mind racing with the weight of the situation. The muggy autumn air warms my skin. The impending trial might not even be our biggest problem. Memories flood my mind—the laughter and camaraderie under the big top, the thrill of each performance, the sense of family that Logan had built for us all. The thought of losing it all makes my chest ache.

When I reach the tent, I pause for a moment to catch my breath before pushing inside. The air inside is thick with tension, performers huddled in large groups, their voices high and worried.

CHAPTER FIVE

I STEP INSIDE, muted colors and dim light creating a heavy, almost oppressive atmosphere. The typical high-spirited energy is replaced by heated arguments, voices clashing like cymbals. Felix is in the center of it all, his hands gesturing wildly as he shouts about taking action.

"That's going to make it worse!" someone counters, their voice sharp with frustration. "We should just move on. He can catch up when he's free."

"If he ever gets free," someone else says.

Ignoring the knot tightening in my stomach, I stride to the center of the big top. I clear my throat, trying to get their attention. No one even glances my way.

"Listen up!" I shout, but my voice is swallowed by the cacophony.

Then I spot Travis, standing off to the side, his arms crossed and a worried expression on his face. Our eyes meet, and for a split second, I'm transported back to our childhood. The boy who once shared secrets and dreams with me but later drifted away under the weight of bullying and fear.

He's changed since joining the circus—stronger, more confident—but there's still a trace of that nervousness in his eyes.

Without a word, he moves toward me.

For a second, I think Travis is going to tell me I don't belong, that he's going to blame me for this predicament, just like Emerson and probably everyone else here. My heart pounds in my chest as he approaches.

Instead, he offers a small, weary smile. "You okay?"

The tension in my shoulders eases a fraction. "I'm holding up."

He nods, looking over his shoulder at the chaos. "It's a mess without Whitmere."

"Yeah," I say, the word coming out on a sigh.

"Do you have any idea what we're going to do?" His voice drops to a whisper, almost lost in the din around us.

I glance around the tent, seeing familiar faces

contorted with worry and anger. Felix is still arguing. Nadia is looking down at her phone… accepting the job offer? The harmony of the circus family has shattered.

"I don't know yet," I admit, hating the uncertainty in my voice.

Travis's gaze shifts to the ground, and he kicks at an invisible pebble. "They're scared, Sienna. We're all scared."

"We need to stay strong for Logan. He's counting on us."

"And what if we can't?" His voice trembles slightly, eyes meeting mine with raw vulnerability. "It's easy for you, because you've always been strong."

I snort. "I just haven't had any other choice."

Travis studies me and then nods. He turns away and cups his hands around his mouth. His piercing whistle that echoes off the heavy canvas walls.

Arguments halt abruptly. Heads snap toward us.

I take a deep breath, steeling myself for what's to come. The eyes of the entire circus crew bore into me, a mix of curiosity, skepticism, and outright hostility.

"We're staying here," I announce, hoping I

sound stronger than I feel.

Nadia steps forward. "We need to perform. Not sit around."

"That's why we're going to create a new show while we wait for Logan to be cleared."

The silence that follows is deafening. Then, all at once, voices erupt.

"Who put you in charge?" Felix snaps, his eyes narrowing. "We signed up to follow Logan, not take orders from some townie."

"You're right. You did sign up to follow him. And that's exactly why we're going to create the best damn show this circus has ever seen." I pause, letting my gaze sweep across the faces before me. "Logan built this circus from nothing. He gave each of us a home when the rest of the world turned its back. Now it's our turn to fight for him."

"And how's a show gonna help?" someone calls out.

"It'll keep us together," I say, my voice gaining strength. "It'll show this town—and Logan— that we're not going anywhere. That we're stronger than their prejudices and their small-minded fears."

I see Travis nodding, a small smile on his face. It gives me courage.

"I'm not performing for these assholes," someone shouts.

"Then we don't," I say. "We put the tickets online. If the circus can't go to them, then we bring them to the circus." I take a deep breath. "Logan's given everything for this circus. For us. Now it's our turn to give back. We're not just performers—we're a family. And family doesn't abandon each other when things get tough."

The tension in the tent shifts, like the air pressure before a storm.

"So who's with me?" I ask, my heart pounding. "Who's ready to show this town what the Cirque des Miroirs is really made of?"

"I'm out." Nadia looks sad about it at least, but she shakes her head.

"Wait. Please."

Her dark eyes turn to me. "I'm sorry, townie. I understand what you're trying to do here. I even respect it, but I can't risk my career. Better to get out now when the offers are coming in than go begging for scraps when he gets convicted of murder."

Her words stab me. "That's not going to happen."

She shrugs a slender shoulder and walks out of the tent.

There's a moment of silence as everyone processes her exit.

She'll be the first of many, the domino that ends this circus forever.

Unless I can find some way to stop it, some magic words.

I take a deep breath, my chest heavy beneath the weight of their stares. Nadia's exit has left a gaping hole in our ranks, and I can see the uncertainty rippling through the crowd. I need to act fast before we lose anyone else.

"Listen," I say, my voice steady despite the tremor in my hands. "I know you're scared. We all are. But Logan didn't build this circus by running away when things got tough."

There's slow clapping from behind the crowd.

They move aside, revealing Emerson. Wolfgang is with him. Who knows how long they've been back there after breaking up the fight. It's clear they heard some of what I've said. The ringmaster's expression is disdainful.

"Well, well," he drawls, his voice dripping with sarcasm. "Look at our little fortune teller, trying to tell everyone's fortune at once."

I straighten my spine, refusing to be cowed. "I'm just trying to—"

"To what?" he cuts me off, striding forward.

"To play ringmaster? To take my place? You can have it, sweetheart. It's yours."

His words sting, but I force myself to hold my ground. "That's not what this is about."

Emerson's laugh is sharp and humorless. "Oh, isn't it? You have no idea how Logan built this circus because you weren't here. You didn't see the blood, sweat, and tears we poured into it."

Everyone's gazes dart between Emerson and me.

"I'm not trying to replace you or Logan or anyone. I'm trying to keep his circus together until he gets out."

Emerson's eyes narrow. "And who gave you that right? You're just a townie who stumbled into our world. You have no authority here."

Emerson's eyes blaze with an intensity that makes my breath catch. He steps forward, commanding the space with a presence I can only dream of possessing. He turns to face the crowd, arms spread, revealing the same magnetism that makes him such an effective ringmaster.

"She wants to talk about family," he begins, his voice low and resonant, yet it carries to every corner of the tent. "What family? She's not part of this."

A hush falls over the crowd, drawn in by his

charisma. Their focus shifts from me to him, their faith realigning with the man who has led them through countless performances.

"She's going to drive us into the ground with her half-baked plans and misplaced loyalty." Emerson paces with a predatory grace. "I, for one, am not sticking around to watch it happen." He pauses, letting each word sink in. "I suggest you all leave as well."

I watch, small and insignificant next to his grandeur. His tailored suit moves fluidly with each step, the red and black fabric almost alive under the dim lights.

"And yes," he says, his eyes locking on to mine for a brief moment before sweeping over the crowd again, "Logan is in trouble. He got himself into trouble. By being in lust for a townie. By being pussy-whipped."

There's some grumbling in the crowd, some agreement and some disagreement.

He sweeps his arm dramatically. "Well, Logan may be pussy-whipped but I'm not."

There's a murmur of agreement rippling through the crowd, and my heart sinks further. How can I compete with this? His words are like honeyed poison—irresistible yet dangerous.

"Logan doesn't just own this circus. He *is* the

circus," Emerson says, his voice swelling with conviction. "Which means it doesn't exist until he gets out."

Felix nods, his earlier anger replaced by reluctant agreement.

Even Travis looks swayed, his posture more tense.

My resolve crumbles bit by bit. How can I lead when I can't even command their attention like he does? Emerson's eloquence makes me feel like an imposter in my own skin.

He turns back to me, a sly smile playing on his lips. "So tell me, Sienna," he asks, "do you have Logan hiding in your pockets?"

I swallow hard, the weight of their gazes pressing down on me like a physical force. Words fail me. They stick in my throat like glue.

Emerson waits, one eyebrow raised in mocking curiosity.

The silence stretches unbearably.

In that moment, I realize how outmatched I am. Emerson isn't just a ringmaster—he's a maestro of words and emotions, orchestrating our lives with effortless finesse.

I don't have that kind of power.

And it terrifies me.

"I didn't think so," he says, sounding disappointed.

Then he turns in a whirl of graceful male and leaves.

The silence that follows is deafening. I can see the uncertainty on everyone's faces, the fear and doubt defeating any hope. Emerson's words have struck a chord. I realize with a sinking heart that I've lost them.

I lock eyes with Felix, remembering that he lived on the streets before he joined the circus. "Felix, remember when Logan found you? You were sleeping under a bridge, right? He didn't just give you a job, he gave you a home."

Felix's hostile expression softens slightly, and I press on.

I realize I didn't need the magic words. It's not about saying anything. It's about *doing* something, and Logan has changed every life here. Including mine.

All I have to do is remind them of that.

"And Cat," I turn to the young woman who made herself my enemy, who almost got me killed. "I know Logan cares about you. It's one of the reasons he took over the circus when your mother was in trouble."

Cat nods, her eyes turning sad.

"Travis," I say, turning to my old friend.

"Logan gave you a chance when our hometown wouldn't. He saw your talent when everyone else just saw…" I trail off, not wanting to bring up painful memories.

Travis finishes for me, his voice quiet but firm. "When they just saw a queer kid who didn't fit in."

A lump forms in my throat. "Logan's done this for all of us. He's taken in ex-cons, runaways, misfits. He didn't just give us jobs. He gave us a family. And now, when he needs us most, are we really going to abandon him?"

The tent falls silent, the weight of my words hanging in the air. I can see the conflict on their faces, the battle between fear and loyalty.

"You're more than just performers," I continue, my voice growing stronger. "You're a family. I might not be one of you, but family doesn't give up on each other when things get tough. You stick together, you fight together, and you sure as hell don't let one of your own rot in jail while you run away."

CHAPTER SIX

FELIX IS THE first to break the silence. "You're right," he says, his voice gruff but sincere. "Logan gave me a chance when no one else would. I owe him everything."

I hold my breath, scanning the faces around me. The tension in the air is palpable, but something's shifting.

Cat nods, her eyes shining with determination. "Me too. I wouldn't be here without him."

One by one, voices join in, a chorus of agreement rising like a wave.

"Logan believed in me when I didn't believe in myself," Travis says, his voice stronger than I've ever heard it.

The energy in the tent is changing, skepticism giving way to resolve. I can see it in their eyes, the way they stand a little straighter, shoulders squared.

"So what's the plan?" someone calls out.

I take a deep breath. "We create the most spectacular show this town has ever seen. We remind them why they loved the circus in the first place."

Ideas start flying. Trapeze artists suggest new routines, clowns brainstorm fresh acts. Even the stagehands chime in with ways to make the show more dazzling.

The enthusiasm is contagious. I watch as the crew, once divided and uncertain, comes together with a shared purpose. They're no longer just performers going through the motions; they're a family fighting for one of their own. In fact I think that's partly why they were fighting; they *need* to do something. Sitting around will make any of us go crazy.

As the brainstorming continues, I catch Travis's eye. He gives me a small nod, a silent acknowledgment of what we've accomplished.

The circus isn't just surviving. It's coming alive with renewed passion and determination. And in this moment, I know we have a chance. Not just to save Logan, but to show this town— and ourselves—what the Cirque des Miroirs is truly made of.

The flap of the tent rustles, I glance up to see Maisie walking in, her face lighting up when she spots me. But it's the tiny ball of fur in her arms that makes me grin.

Tricks bounds toward me, his little legs moving fast until he leaps into my arms, his tail wagging furiously.

"There you are," I murmur, burying my face in his soft fur. He licks my cheeks with fervor, his tiny tongue warm against my skin. I laugh through my tears, clutching him close. For a moment, everything else fades away—the tension, the fear, the uncertainty.

Maisie kneels beside me, her hand resting on my shoulder. "What can I do to help?"

I pull back slightly, still holding Tricks but meeting Maisie's eyes. The weight of everything crashes down on me all at once—the responsibility, the fear of failing Logan and everyone else here.

I brief her on the new show.

"I don't know if I can do this," I whisper, my voice cracking under the strain of keeping it together.

Maisie's expression softens, and she squeezes my shoulder. "Sienna, you have more heart than anyone I've ever known."

Her words hit me like a gentle wave, soothing but insistent. She's always been the one to believe in me when I couldn't believe in myself.

"But what if that's not enough?"

Maisie tilts her head slightly, giving me that expression she always does when she's about to say something profound. "Heart isn't enough—it's everything. It's what makes you fight for Logan and this circus even when things seem impossible."

Hope rises in me. Tricks wriggles in my arms, reminding me of all the love and loyalty that still exists here—despite everything.

Maisie continues, "You're not alone in this. We're all here for you and for Logan. And you've got Tricks here to remind you of that every step of the way."

Tricks squirms in my arms, licking my chin, as if reminding me that there's still joy to be found even in the darkest moments.

I clutch him a little tighter. "Thank you. And, Maisie, we're *really* going to need that social media stuff. Because we also have tickets to sell."

Maisie's head tilts. "You don't think Forrester will buy them?"

"I don't know, but the circus doesn't want to perform for the people who are responsible for locking up Logan. And I understand that, actually."

Maisie nods, her eyes filled with determination. "You're right. In fact, this might even help us. We won't just sell the tickets. We'll auction them off. We can use this to build buzz for Logan's situation. A cause is much easier to support if it comes with skintight leotards and triple backflips."

I glance around the tent, where our makeshift family is beginning to rally together despite their doubts. "This just might work," I say softly. "Maybe they needed this. Maybe I did, too."

She looks at me, and I can see the same fire in her eyes that's burning in mine. "We won't auction all the tickets, though. We'll save some for giveaways. Get a few minor celebrities interested. Let them use their platforms to get the word out about small-town corruption."

"Yeah." A small spark of hope ignites inside me again. "So it's not just about the show, not even for the people attending. They'll know what's at stake, too."

Maisie smiles softly, brushing a strand of hair from my face. "You've got this."

Wolfgang's imposing figure suddenly looms over us.

His eyes narrow as they land on Maisie. "What's she doing here?"

I open my mouth to defend her, but Maisie beats me to it.

"I'm here to support my friend," she says, her voice steady despite Wolfgang's intimidating presence. "Which is more than I can say for you. Why are you always around when you're not wanted?"

Wow. Maisie never talks like that. To anyone.

Wolfgang's jaw clenches. "You're a townie. You don't belong here. This is circus land, and you're on the enemy side now."

Tricks tenses in my arms. Maisie, however, doesn't back down. She stands taller, her petite frame somehow filling the space between us.

"Enemy side?" she scoffs. "I'm here for Sienna. And Logan. If that makes me an enemy, then your priorities are seriously messed up."

Wolfgang takes a step closer, towering over Maisie. "You could be spying for the sheriff. Who knows? You need to leave. Now."

To my surprise, Maisie doesn't flinch. Instead, she tilts her chin up, meeting Wolfgang's glare head-on. "Make me," she challenges. "Throw me out if you dare."

"You think I won't?"

It should be laughable, this tiny blonde standing up to a muscled knife thrower. But there's something in Maisie's stance, a fire in her eyes that makes her seem invincible.

Maisie crosses her arms. "I think you know Sienna needs all the support she can get right now. And if you *actually* care about that, you'll focus on the new show instead of being an asshole."

Wolfgang's eyes linger on Maisie's face a beat too long. Maisie's cheeks flush pink. Could they be… interested in each other? The thought seems absurd at first, but the heated exchange doesn't make sense otherwise.

"Fine, but if I catch you causing trouble…"

Maisie rolls her eyes. "Please. I'm not the one with the problem here."

Hang on a freaking second.

The tension, the spark between them…

It's perfect.

"I've got it," I blurt out, interrupting their bickering.

They both turn to face me.

"Got what?" Wolfgang says on a grunt.

"The theme for the new show," I explain, excitement bubbling up inside me. "It's going to be centered around romance. Based on *Romeo and*

Juliet, but with a circus twist. We'll call it 'Star-Crossed.'"

Maisie's face lights up immediately. "That's brilliant, Sienna! It's perfect for showcasing the circus acts while having universal appeal. The internet is going to eat this up with a spoon."

Wolfgang, on the other hand, looks dubious. His brow furrows as he crosses his arms over his chest. "*Romeo and Juliet*? Isn't it kind of... sad?"

"Not the way we're going to do it," I counter, my mind already whirling with possibilities. "We'll use the circus acts to tell the story in a way no one's ever seen before. Trapeze for the balcony scene, knife throwing for the fight sequences..."

As I speak, I can see the gears turning in Wolfgang's head. He's still skeptical, but there's a glimmer of interest in his eyes.

"Don't worry. I'll show you," I say, scooping up my little dog. "Come on, Tricks. We've got a lot of work to do."

CHAPTER SEVEN

I STEP INTO the jailhouse.

The reception lady looks up from her desk, her eyes narrowing as she spots me. Her lips curl into a sneer, but she picks up the phone and mutters something I can't make out.

Moments later, a deputy appears, motioning for me to follow. Instead of heading toward the cells, though, I veer off to the sheriff's office. The deputy opens his mouth to protest, but I push past him, determination fueling my every step.

Sheriff Dunham is behind his desk, feet propped up like he owns the world. He leans back in his chair, eyes roaming over me with a leer that makes my skin crawl.

"Well, if it isn't Miss Cole," he drawls. "To what do I owe the pleasure?"

I force myself to stand tall, locking eyes with

him. "I want to know why there's been a delay in Logan's bail."

He chuckles, the sound low and mocking. "Oh, sweetheart, you really think it's that simple?"

"Don't call me sweetheart," I snap. "And yes, I do think it's that simple. The evidence against him is flimsy at best."

His smile widens, but there's no warmth in it. "Flimsy? We've got his fingerprints on a crowbar covered in blood."

My hands clench into fists at my sides. "That evidence was planted. By you."

He shrugs nonchalantly. "Doesn't matter what you think happened. What matters is what the court thinks."

"Then why delay bail? If you're so confident in your case?"

His eyes darken, and he leans forward, resting his elbows on the desk. "I'm enjoying watching him squirm. That's reason enough."

My stomach twists at his words. "You have no right—"

"I have every right. This is my town, my rules. Besides, the only prosecutor has been mighty busy. We are a small town, you know." He smirks, making it clear that everyone knows exactly how busy the judge gets when he goes down south past the border, where he can do as much drugs and underage girls as his poor, triple-bypass heart can stand. "I'm sure he'll get around to it."

"Wait much longer and it'll be considered a breach of his due process. I'm sure you don't want the state attorney general to take an interest in this case."

Sheriff Dunham studies me for a moment, his gaze lingering on my face. I can tell he's weighing his options, trying to decide whether to help me or not. I know he's a corrupt man, but he's also one who understands a threat when he hears one. In a way it's a thin promise. It's not like I can actually make the state attorney general investigate anything. He might, though. Will the sheriff take that risk?

"I'll reach out to him," he says gruffly. "Tell him it's been long enough."

I give him a short nod, because that's all I can do. For now.

As I'm led to the small jail cell, I steel myself for what's to come. Fluorescent lights overhead flicker, casting eerie shadows on the chipped paint of the walls.

When I finally see Logan through the bars, my heart skips a beat.

His dark, tousled hair hangs limply around his chiseled face, his eyes haunted, like those of a hunted animal. His white shirt is tossed across the small, stained cot. That leaves him shirtless. The intricate tattoos that snake across his biceps and shoulders seem to writhe in the dim light, telling stories of a hard life. And of hope.

My eyes well up with tears at the sight of him, the man I love, caged like some exotic creature in this godforsaken place. But I push the emotions down, forcing a brave smile to my lips. I can't let him see how much this is killing me.

Wolfgang is already inside. They're speaking in low, serious tones.

When he sees me, he nods and steps past me.

The solid metal door closes behind me with a thud.

Logan stands on the other side of the bars, his eyes weary and haunted. Seeing him like this, my heart sinks. I take a deep breath, willing myself to put on a brave face. He needs my strength right now, not my tears.

The cell reeks of despair and old sweat.

The tattoos are a vibrant tapestry of circus scenes, painted with an artist's precision. On one shoulder, acrobats soar through the air, their limbs elongated in impossible grace. Below them, a ringmaster cracks his whip, his face contorted in a mixture of glee and menace. On Logan's chest, a contortionist bends in ways that defy human anatomy, her eyes wide and hauntingly beautiful.

But not all of it is playful. There are grotesque images too. A clown with jagged teeth grins malevolently from his left bicep, while a strongman lifts an impossibly heavy barbell with veins bulging from his neck. The vibrant colors of the tattoos seem almost out of place in this drab, gray cell.

A thin sheen of sweat glistens on Logan's skin, highlighting the definition of his muscles. Each curve tells a story of hard work and dedication, but also pain and sacrifice. His broad shoulders look capable of carrying the weight of the world—or at least the weight of this damn circus.

He looks up as I approach, eyes locking on to mine. Despite the haunted light in them, he's still undeniably hot. His presence fills the small space, making it less like a cage and more like... something else.

The heavy growth on his face, not quite a beard, but more than faint scruff, makes him seem even more dangerous, like a caged circus animal.

"Hey," I say softly, stepping closer to the bars.

He looks up, a shadow of a smile flickering

across his lips. "Hey yourself."

I reach out, my fingers curling around the cold metal. "How are you holding up?"

Logan's shoulders sag, and he lets out a heavy sigh. "Wolfgang was just telling me about what happened."

The words hit me like a punch to the gut. "I hate that you have to worry about this."

He blows out a breath. "I know that Nadia leaving is a bigger blow to the circus, but somehow Emerson leaving hurts worse."

"We'll manage," I say, though my voice wavers slightly.

He shakes his head, his eyes filled with defeat. "It's falling apart, Sienna. Everything I've worked for… It's slipping through my fingers."

"Hey," I say firmly, trying to inject some steel into my voice. "We are not giving up. We'll figure this out."

Logan's gaze locks on to mine, and for a moment, his severe expression softens. "How do you do it? How do you stay so strong?"

I force a smile. "It was that or die."

A ghost of a chuckle escapes his lips. "You always were a tough one."

"Takes one to know one," I shoot back, hoping to lighten the mood even just a little.

But his expression turns serious again, the weight of our situation pressing down on him. "I don't want you visiting me here anymore," he says suddenly.

The words hit me harder than any blow Kyle ever dealt me. "What? Why?"

"I can't stand seeing you like this," he admits, his voice cracking. "It's tearing me apart."

"I'm not leaving you," I say fiercely, gripping the bars tighter. "You hear me? I'm not going anywhere."

His hand reaches through the bars, touching mine briefly before pulling away as if burned by the contact. "Sienna…"

"Don't," I interrupt him. "Don't push me away now."

He looks at me with those haunted eyes, and I can see the internal battle he's fighting—wanting to protect me but needing me close.

I grip the bars so tightly my knuckles turn white. "This isn't fair, Logan. You don't deserve to be in here."

His eyes darken, and he looks down at his feet. "Fairness has nothing to do with it, Sienna. They're out to get me because I stood up to them."

"But you did it for me," I whisper, my voice

trembling. "This is all my fault."

He shakes his head sharply. "Don't you dare think that. I made my choices."

My throat tightens as I fight back tears. "The evidence… Logan, they're saying they have your fingerprints on the crowbar. It's bullshit."

"I know. But proving that is another story."

"The lawyer's working on it." I try to inject some hope into my words.

Logan's eyes meet mine again, filled with a mix of desperation and determination. "It's not even about the murder charge. It's about these fucking bars. About being chained up. Watched. Mocked. About being like my father."

My heart drops to the pit of my stomach. Logan feels like he's become his father, the circus freak, the criminal, the rapist. The very thing he's spent his life trying to escape, now shackling him tighter than any set of bars ever could.

"No," I breathe out, the word escaping my lips before I can stop it. "Logan, you're nothing like him."

His eyes flash with pain and anger. "Aren't I? Look at me, Sienna. Look at where I am."

I step closer to the bars, wanting to reach out, to hold him, to break through this invisible wall of despair that's crushing him. "Your father… He was a monster in human form. You're not."

Logan's laugh is bitter and hollow. "And what am I now? A caged animal for people to gawk at?"

"Stop it," I say fiercely. "You're Logan Whitmere. The man who saved me from a life of misery. The man who built a home for outcasts, who gave them purpose and pride."

He shakes his head, looking away from me, as if ashamed. "I feel like him every time these bars clang shut behind me."

My chest tightens with the weight of his words. Seeing him like this—broken, dehumanized—it's unbearable.

"Logan," I whisper, my voice trembling. "This place… It's temporary. We'll get you out."

He finally meets my gaze again, his eyes searching mine for something—hope, maybe, or reassurance. "And what then? What if they drag me back? What if this is my life now?"

"No," I say firmly, trying to pour every ounce of conviction into my words. "We won't let that happen."

A tear slips down my cheek, and I quickly brush it away. "You're not your father. You never were and you never will be."

His jaw clenches, and he closes his eyes briefly as if trying to block out the truth of our situation.

"I just… don't want you to see me like this," he mutters.

"Too late," I reply softly but with steel in my voice. "I've already seen you at your worst and your best, Logan. And I'm still here."

He opens his eyes again, something softening in his expression.

"We'll get through this," I promise him.

Logan looks at me with a mixture of gratitude and sadness, but there's a flicker of something else too—a spark of hope.

It's small, but it's enough for now.

"Just… don't give up," I whisper.

I glance toward the door and spot the back of Wolfgang's head through the tiny window. No nosy deputies in sight, either. Before I can second-guess myself, I reach through the bars and grab Logan's hand. His fingers curl around mine instantly, a lifeline in this hellish place.

His touch is warm and strong, grounding me in this moment of chaos. I squeeze his hand tightly, pouring every ounce of love and support into that simple gesture.

"We'll get through this," I say.

Logan's grip tightens in response.

I study the gorgeous tapestry of tattoos across his body—the red-and-white striped circus tent, the lion standing up on his back paws, the carousel with its macabre faces. My eyebrows pull together. It almost looks darker beneath the flame-covered ring.

I'm unfortunately very familiar with bruises like that, the kind made with fists.

"What happened?" I ask, my pulse thudding in my ears.

He looks grim and sardonic. "I tripped."

"On what? There's barely anything in there."

"It doesn't matter."

"It does freaking matter if they're abusing you. You're a prisoner here. You have rights. We can call Harrison. Or the ACLU. Or the newspapers. Or—"

"We're not calling anyone."

"Logan—"

"Stop."

The air between us crackles, charged with an intensity that sends a shiver down my spine. Logan's gaze holds mine, a mix of desperation and desire swirling in those stormy eyes. Heat radiates off his body, drawing me in like a moth to a flame. My breath hitches, caught in the moment, as our emotions run high and wild.

His voice is low, almost a growl, when he speaks. "You shouldn't even be here."

I step closer to the bars, the metal emanating cold. "Yes, I should."

His eyes flash. "You don't know what you're doing to me."

My heart pounds with a primal rhythm. "And what is that?"

His gaze roams over me, lingering on the curves of my body. I can feel the weight of his stare, like a physical touch, setting my nerves alight. The tension between us is palpable, a taut wire ready to snap.

Something shifts in his expression. His eyes turn cruel, a harsh gleam replacing the heat from moments before. My stomach twists, a sense of unease washing over me.

"I've been hard up in here," he says, his voice cold and distant. "If you're so intent on comforting me, how about putting on a little show?"

The words hit me like a slap, a brutal reminder of the walls he's trying to build between us. I can see it in his eyes—he wants to push me away, to use sex as a weapon, a barrier to keep me at arm's length.

And after being taunted and shamed by the town for years, it's working.

Logan's words hang in the air, a brutal challenge that cuts deep. "Show me somethin' pretty if you want to stick around." His eyes, once warm and inviting, now glint with a cruel edge. My heart hammers against my ribs, a drumbeat of confusion and hurt.

Part of me wants to run, to flee this cold, harsh version of the man I love. But another part, a darker, more insidious part, wonders if this is all I'm good for. The echoes of Kyle's taunts, the whispers of the town, all swirl in my mind. "Trash." "Worthless." "Good for nothing but a quick lay."

I stand there, frozen, my breath coming in shallow gasps. Logan's gaze bores into me, waiting, demanding. His lips curl into a smirk, a cruel mockery of his usual smile. It's like he's become a stranger, a dark reflection of the man I know.

"Well?" he prompts, his voice a low growl. "What's it gonna be, Sienna?"

My hands tremble as I reach for the hem of my shirt, a sense of dread washing over me. Is this what I've been reduced to? A performance, a spectacle for his amusement? But if it means staying with him, if it means not losing him completely…

I hesitate, my fingers toying with the fabric. Logan's eyes follow the movement, a hungry gleam in their depths. It's a hunger I recognize, but it's tainted now, twisted into something ugly and wrong.

"Logan," I whisper, a plea in my voice. "Don't do this."

His smirk fades, replaced by a hard, unyielding expression. "You wanted to stay, Sienna. This is the price."

Tears sting my eyes, blurring my vision. I blink them back, refusing to let them fall. I won't cry, not in front of him. Not like this.

My hands drop to my sides, my resolve crumbling. I can't do it. I can't debase myself like this, not even for him.

"I… I can't," I choke out, my voice barely a whisper.

Logan's expression doesn't change, but something in his eyes flickers. A hint of regret, perhaps, or maybe it's just my imagination, a desperate attempt to find the man I love in this cold, cruel stranger.

I take a step back, my heart heavy with defeat. "I'm sorry, Logan. I can't do this."

His jaw clenches, a muscle twitching in his cheek. For a moment, he says nothing, his gaze locked on to mine. Then, he turns away, his shoulders tense, his back rigid.

"Fine," he says, his voice cold and distant. "Then go."

CHAPTER EIGHT

I PAUSE, MY hand on the cold metal door, ready to walk away. But I can't. Not like this. Logan needs me, even if it's in this twisted, fucked-up way. I take a deep breath, steeling myself, and pull my top over my head. The fabric whispers against my skin, a soft sigh in the harsh silence of the jail cell.

Logan turns to face me, his green eyes dark and intense. A shiver runs down my spine, a primal response to the hunger in his gaze. "Show me your tits, Sienna," he commands, his voice a low growl that seems to resonate in the very air between us.

I glance nervously at the door, my heart pounding in my chest. Logan follows my gaze, a cruel smirk playing at the corners of his mouth. "No one's coming in here," he says, a cold certainty in his voice. "Not while Wolfgang's out there."

My hands tremble as I reach behind my back, unclasping my bra. The cool air brushes over my nipples, making them harden, a physical betrayal of the turmoil inside me. I let the bra fall to the floor, my breath coming in shallow gasps.

Logan's eyes roam over me, a hungry, feral look. It's more than just the emotion of being jailed that's dehumanizing him. He's becoming more primal, a creature of raw, unbridled need.

"Hold them up for me," he orders, his voice a harsh rasp. I hesitate, a blush spreading across my cheeks. Embarrassment wars with something darker, something more insidious. A part of me wants to obey, to submit to his cold commands, to bask in the heat of his gaze.

I cup my breasts, lifting them, offering them to his hungry eyes. His gaze is like a physical touch, setting my nerves alight, sending a rush of heat between my legs. I'm wet, my body responding to his demands, to the bulge in his slacks that betrays his own arousal.

"Pinch the tips," he growls, his eyes never leaving my body. I comply, a gasp escaping my lips as I roll the hardened peaks between my fingers. The sensation is intense, a mix of pleasure and pain that sends a jolt of electricity straight to my core.

I stand there, my body on display, my cheeks flushed with embarrassment and arousal. Logan's eyes are dark, his breath coming in harsh pants. The air between us is charged, a taut wire ready to snap. And despite the fucked-up nature of it all, I can't deny the heat coursing through my veins, the wetness between my thighs. I'm turned on, my body responding to his primal need, to the raw, unbridled hunger in his gaze.

Logan's voice is a dark rumble, like distant thunder. "My father used to do this. Even back then, when women barely knew about sex, without the internet, without videos, women would come, pay a quarter to see the tattooed freak. He'd give them orders in the dark, just like this. They'd show their tits."

I shudder, my breath hitching. "Logan, don't—"

"Lick your fingertips," he commands, his eyes never leaving mine. I hesitate, then comply, my tongue darting out to wet the tips of my fingers. "Now, moisten your nipples."

I do as he says, the sensation sending a shiver down my spine. His gaze is intense, burning into me. "He'd lure them to the back of the tent after the show. Rape them."

"Logan, you're not him," I whisper, my voice barely audible.

He laughs, a sharp, bitter sound. "Aren't I? You're showing your body to a man just like him, Sienna." His voice is cold, cruel. "Now, keep that pretty mouth shut unless you want something stuffed inside it."

I gasp, his words a slap in the face. But beneath the shock, there's a dark, twisted part of me that responds to his crude command. I press my lips together, my eyes locked on to his, waiting for his next order. The air between us is thick with tension, a charged silence that crackles with a dark, forbidden energy.

His voice cuts through the silence, a harsh command. "Unbutton your jeans, Sienna. Slip your hand down. Touch yourself."

My breath hitches, but I don't hesitate. My fingers fumble with the button, the zipper, eager to obey. I push my hand past the waistband, down into the damp heat between my thighs. A gasp escapes my lips as I find my clit, swollen and sensitive.

"That's it," Logan growls, his voice a low rumble that vibrates through me. "Rub it for me, Sunset. Let me see you chase that feeling."

My fingers move in tight circles, the sensation intense, electric. I'm wet, so wet, my body responding to his commands, to the raw need in his voice. I lean back against the cold wall, my hips arching, seeking more.

Logan's eyes are locked on me, his breath coming in harsh pants. He's with me, even though he's locked behind those bars. We're connected, our desires intertwined, our bodies syncing in this fucked-up dance.

"Imagine it's me," he rasps. "My fingers on you, my tongue. Imagine me fucking you, Sienna. Hard and deep, just like you need."

A moan escapes my lips, my body clenching at his words. I'm not in the jail anymore. I'm somewhere else, somewhere wild and free. It's just Logan and me, our bodies moving together, our breaths mingling, our hearts pounding in sync.

My fingers move faster, the pressure building. I'm close, so close. Logan's voice is a distant rumble, urging me on, pushing me higher. "Come for me, Sienna," he growls. "Let me see you come."

And I do. The orgasm rips through me, a wave of intense pleasure that leaves me gasping, my body convulsing. I ride it out, my fingers slowing, my breath coming in ragged gasps.

Time seems to stand still as I reach my climax, my body trembling with a mix of pleasure and emotional release. A gasp catches in my throat, my fingers pressing hard against my clit, riding out the waves that crash through me. Logan's eyes bore into me, his breath ragged, matching my own panting breaths.

I lean against the cold wall, my body still convulsing with the remnants of my orgasm. Logan's voice, a low growl, cuts through the haze. "Show me your fingers, Sienna. Let me see how wet you are."

I pull my hand from my jeans, my fingers glistening with my arousal. I hold them up, a shiver running down my spine as Logan's eyes darken. He reaches through the bars, his hand wrapping around my wrist, pulling me closer.

"You're so fucking sexy, Sunset," he rasps. A jolt of electricity shoots through me, my body responding to the raw, primal words.

"You're mine," he growls, his voice a low rumble that seems to resonate in the very air between us. "No matter what happens, even when I'm locked up, that hot little body belongs to me, doesn't it?"

I nod, my voice catching in my throat. "Yours," I whisper, the word a promise, a vow.

No matter the distance, no matter the bars between us, I belong to Logan Whitmere. And he belongs to me.

My heart swells with a mix of longing. And determination. He's a handsome, rugged man, but there's a loneliness in his eyes that calls to me. My gaze drifts down, admiring the size of his bulge, imagining his cock inside me, filling me completely. I bite my lip, a shiver of anticipation running down my spine.

"Can you… come too?" I ask, my voice barely a whisper.

"No, not here," he growls, his voice a low rumble that vibrates through me. "I'm saving it for you, Sienna. For when I can have you completely. For when I can come in that delicious little cunt."

A thrill courses through me at his words, a promise of more, of a future together. For even that slightest hint of hope.

Logan's eyes lock on to mine, a fierce intensity burning in their depths. "Let me taste you," he says, his voice a low command that sends a wave of heat crashing through me. I comply, my fingers still glistening with my arousal. He takes my hand, his grip firm, and sucks my fingers into his mouth.

The sensation is intense, electric. I watch, my breath coming in shallow gasps as his tongue swirls around my fingertips, licking them clean. A moan escapes my lips, the sensation intense, intimate. I shiver as he sucks my fingertips, wringing out one last drop of my pleasure. It's more than just a physical act; it's a claim, a promise. I'm his, and he's mine. No bars, no distance can change that.

I tremble, my breath coming in ragged gasps as Logan releases me. His eyes meet mine, a storm of emotion swirling in their depths. I stand there, my heart pounding, my body aching for more.

I can't have more.

Not now.

Maybe not ever.

I straighten my clothes, the weight of reality settling back onto my shoulders. My fingers tremble as I adjust my bra and pull my shirt down, trying to regain some semblance of normalcy. Logan's eyes never leave me, watching with a mix of longing and sorrow. I can't stand the thought of leaving him here, behind these cold, unforgiving bars.

"Stay strong for me," Logan murmurs, his voice a soft caress that soothes the raw edges of my heart. "You'll get through this. Whatever happens to me."

I swallow hard to push back the tears threatening to spill. "Don't talk like that," I whisper back, my voice barely audible. "You're going to get out of here."

Logan's hand reaches through the bars, his fingers brushing against mine in a fleeting touch that sends shivers down my spine. "You need to be careful," he warns, his tone shifting to one of concern. "These people are animals."

And they want to make him into an animal, too.

"I won't let them win," I say.

He gives me a small, sad smile that doesn't quite reach his eyes. "They already have, Sunset."

"I'm not giving up on you."

Logan's gaze darkens. "I'll pull you down with me, then."

"I have to go," I finally say, my voice cracking slightly as I take a step back.

Logan nods slowly, his gaze already turned away.

With a heavy heart and one last glance at the man I love, I turn and walk away from the jail cell. The metal door closes behind me with a finality that echoes in my chest, but I carry Logan's dark words with me.

My body still hums from his commands.

It was wrong, the way he spoke to me, but it was also right.

I wasn't talking to the confident man who protected me from bullies before he even knew my name. I was talking to the shadow that's lived inside him since he was born, the one who grew up ashamed, the one who always saw himself as a freak.

As much as I wish he didn't feel that way, I also know that's part of him. And if I love him, I love both the light and the dark.

Those erotic orders were meant to push me away.

Instead they only strengthened my resolve.

CHAPTER NINE

THE COURTROOM BUZZES with low murmurs and the shuffling of papers. I sit in the back, my heart hammering against my ribs as I wait for Logan's bail hearing to begin. The wooden bench beneath me feels cold and unforgiving, mirroring the icy dread seeping into my bones. Faces blur together, a sea of indifferent expressions and judgmental stares. I tug at the sleeves of my denim jacket, seeking some comfort in the familiar fabric.

Sheriff Dunham sits near the front, a smug grin plastered on his face. He catches my eye and winks, making my skin crawl. My threats worked; Logan's getting a hearing. But Dunham's confidence gnaws at me, planting seeds of doubt. The sheriff leans back in his chair, whispering something to a deputy that makes them both chuckle.

Logan deserves this chance to come home until the trial. To breathe fresh air, feel sunlight on his skin again. I can't stand the thought of him trapped in that cell any longer.

A door opens, and Logan is led into the courtroom, handcuffed but standing tall. My breath catches at the sight of him—still strong, still defiant despite everything.

Logan steps into the courtroom, and for a moment, I forget to breathe. He's had a shower, and he's wearing a fresh suit. The fabric clings to his muscular frame in all the right ways, the crisp lines accentuating his broad shoulders and narrow waist. His face is clean-shaven, not a single shadow marring his strong jawline. He looks completely put together, almost like the Logan I know from the circus—proud, unbreakable.

Except for his eyes.

They're haunted, those deep pools of stormy gray. Shadows linger there, a darkness that speaks of sleepless nights and relentless torment. I see the toll this place has taken on him, the silent battles he's fighting behind those bars. My chest tightens as I catch his gaze. For a brief second, something flickers in his eyes—a mix of pain and relief.

Logan's eyes scan the room and settle on me. I

try to muster a reassuring smile, but it's brittle on my lips. He gives a barely perceptible nod, acknowledging my presence without drawing too much attention.

I give him what I hope is a reassuring smile. *Stay strong.*

The judge enters, commanding silence with his presence alone. Everyone rises, then sits again as he takes his seat. My fingers clench around the edge of the bench as the hearing begins.

I watch as a middle-aged man in an expensive suit rises from his seat. His silver hair is slicked back, and a gold watch glints on his wrist. Kyle's uncle, the prosecutor. My stomach churns as he approaches the judge, exuding an air of smug confidence.

"Your Honor," he begins, his voice dripping with false sincerity, "Logan Whitmere is nothing more than a drifter, a charlatan who preys on small towns like ours with his carnival."

I clench my fists, biting my tongue to keep from calling bullshit.

The words paint a grotesque caricature of the man I love.

"This violent vagrant has no ties to our community, no stable income, and no reason to stay if released on bail. He's a flight risk, pure and simple."

The prosecutor paces before the judge, his polished shoes clicking against the floor. "Mr. Whitmere's history shows a pattern of moving from town to town, never putting down roots. How can we trust he won't disappear the moment he's released?"

I glance at Logan, seeing the muscle in his jaw tighten. His eyes remain fixed ahead, tension radiating from him.

"Furthermore, Your Honor, the nature of the crime is exceptionally violent. A respected member of our community was brutally attacked. Can we really allow such a dangerous individual to roam free among us?"

The prosecutor's voice rises, his gestures becoming more animated. "This man, if we can call him that, lives in a tent. He has no permanent address, no stable job beyond his circus sideshow. He's little more than a bum with delusions of grandeur."

My nails dig into my palms, rage building inside me. The prosecutor's words twist everything into something dirty and shameful.

"Your Honor, I implore you to deny bail. For the safety of our town, for justice, keep this violent drifter behind bars where he belongs."

Alex Harrison stands, his solid presence commanding attention, a stark contrast to the prosecutor's oily charm. "Your Honor," he begins, his voice steady and confident. "I'd like to present a different picture of Logan Whitmere. Far from being a drifter, Mr. Whitmere is a successful businessman who employs hundreds of people and generates significant revenue in every city the Cirque des Miroirs visits."

I watch as the judge leans forward, clearly intrigued. Alex continues, his words painting Logan in the light he deserves.

"Mr. Whitmere isn't just a businessman but a pillar of community support wherever the circus goes. In every city they visit, the Cirque des Miroirs makes substantial donations to local food banks and animal shelters."

Alex produces a stack of papers from his briefcase. "I have here letters from various charities across the country, thanking Mr. Whitmere for his generous contributions."

He begins to read, his voice carrying through the hushed courtroom. "'Dear Mr. Whitmere, your donation has allowed us to feed over 500 families this month...' 'Thanks to the Cirque des Miroirs, our program was able to upgrade our facilities and save dozens more pets.'"

As Alex reads, I sense a shift in the courtroom. The early hostility seems to lessen. Even some of the town's residents who came to gawk are exchanging uneasy glances.

"These are just a few examples of the positive impact Mr. Whitmere has on communities across the nation," Alex says. "These are not the actions of a 'violent vagrant,' but of a compassionate businessman deeply invested in social responsibility and community care."

This is the man I know, the one who quietly helps those in need without seeking recognition.

"…and thanks to Mr. Whitmere's generosity, I was able to start a new life free from abuse," Harrison finishes, his voice resonating through the courtroom.

The prosecutor stands, looking bored. "Objection, Your Honor. These alleged donations are irrelevant to the crime at hand. For all we know, they could be fabricated."

How fucking dare he? The only fabrication here is the evidence against Logan. I can't help but let out a derisive snort, drawing the prosecutor's attention.

His lip curls in disgust as he looks at me. "Perhaps these 'donations' to women's shelters were just payments for services rendered. After all," he says, gesturing toward me, "that must be how he convinced the town slut to run away with his circus."

The courtroom erupts. Harrison's voice booms above the chaos, "Objection! Your Honor, this is slander."

My vision blurs with surprised hurt.

I watch in horror as Logan snaps to his feet, his eyes blazing with a fury I've never seen before. The chains of his handcuffs rattle as he surges forward, muscles taut and ready to spring. For a moment, I forget to breathe.

"Order! Order in the court!" The judge's voice booms, cutting through the chaos. His gavel slams down once, twice, three times. The sharp cracks echo through the room, but Logan remains standing, his gaze fixed on the prosecutor with murderous intent.

The prosecutor's lips curl into a sneer. "See, Your Honor? He's clearly prone to violence. This outburst only proves my point about the danger he poses to our gentle community."

My heart sinks. This is exactly what they wanted—to provoke Logan, to make him appear like the monster they claim he is. I want to tell everyone that they don't understand, that they're twisting everything.

The judge's voice rings out with a steel edge.

"Counselor," he says, fixing the prosecutor with a hard stare, "I will not tolerate such unprofessional behavior in my courtroom. Your derogatory remarks and attempts to provoke the defendant are completely unacceptable."

The smug expression drops from the prosecutor's face, replaced by shock and then a faux sheepish expression.

"You will retract your statement and apologize to Miss Cole immediately. Furthermore, I'm issuing you a formal reprimand. One more outburst like that, and I'll hold you in contempt. Is that clear?"

The prosecutor's face flushes red. "Y-yes, Your Honor. I apologize for my remarks."

I blink, not saying anything because he barely addressed the words to me. The judge turns his attention to Logan, who's still standing. "Mr. Whitmere, please be seated. I understand your reaction, but I need you to remain calm for the duration of these proceedings."

Logan nods stiffly and sits.

I release a long breath.

Town slut. The familiar sting of shame burns through me, but it's quickly overtaken by a surge of anger. How dare he? I'm not that scared little girl anymore, desperate for approval.

Something unexpected washes over me. A strange sense of… indifference? These people, with their small-town judgments and narrow minds—they don't know me. They don't know Logan. I realize their opinions matter far less than I ever thought possible.

My newfound calmness crumbles as the judge speaks.

"Despite the numerous charitable works undertaken by Mr. Whitmere, I must agree that with his successful circus, with its extensive network, he must be considered a flight risk."

Each word is a blow.

"Given Mr. Whitmere's traveling experience, I have no choice but to deny bail."

The gavel falls with a thud that reverberates in my body.

Logan will remain behind bars until the trial. Pain. Resignation. I see it even though his expression is intentionally blank.

As Logan is led past me, our eyes lock. In that moment, the chaos of the courtroom fades away. Without thinking, I reach forward. The deputy escorting him hesitates, caught off guard by my sudden movement.

Logan's lips crash into mine, desperate and

hungry. The kiss is brief but electric, sending shockwaves through my body. His scent envelops me—a mix of sweat, soap, and something uniquely him.

For a fleeting second, we're not in this suffocating courtroom.

We're under the big top, wrapped in each other's arms.

"I love you," I whisper against his mouth.

"That was your first mistake, Sunset," he murmurs back.

Then he's gone, pulled away by the deputy. I watch as they lead him out, my heart shattering with each step he takes. The heavy wooden doors close behind them with a dull thud that echoes through my soul.

I stand there, frozen, as the courtroom empties around me. My lips still tingle from his kiss, a bittersweet reminder of what's been taken from us. Tears blur my vision, but I blink them back furiously.

I can't break down. Not here.

A storm of emotions rages inside me. Sadness threatens to pull me under, imagining Logan back in that cold, lonely cell. I clench my fists, nails digging into my palms. The pain grounds me, gives me focus.

We may have lost this battle, but the war isn't over. Logan needs me to be strong, to keep the circus together. As I finally turn to leave, I catch sight of Kyle's uncle smirking from across the room. His smug face ignites a fresh wave of anger in me. He thinks he's won, and I'm afraid he might be right.

CHAPTER TEN

I LEAN ACROSS the counter, raising my voice. "Mr. Hawkins, I need the security tape from this summer!"

The old man squints at me, his wrinkled hand cupping his ear. "What's that, Sienna? You need a tape measure for plumbers?"

I suppress a groan. Mr. Hawkins is one of the few people in town still willing to speak to me. "I need your security tapes. I think it might show something important. About the murder case."

He leans in closer. "Something to fix a staircase?"

Okay, I'm pretty sure he's only reading lips. Which I guess works if I'm trying to find something around the hardware store.

I point to the ancient-looking device mounted in the corner.

Mr. Hawkins follows my gesture, his eyes widening in recognition. "Oh! The camera! Why didn't you say so?"

"I'm trying to help prove he's innocent."

Understanding finally dawns on Mr. Hawkins's face. "Ah, I see. Well, I'm sorry to disappoint you, Sienna, but that old thing hasn't worked in years."

My heart sinks. "Are you sure? We could check."

He shakes his head firmly. "Broke down back in oh eight. Never got around to fixing it. It's just for show now, keeps the riffraff thinking they're being watched."

I slump against the counter, disappointment washing over me.

Another dead end.

I'm not sure what the tape would show, really. My father drunkenly leaving the bar, perhaps holding up a sign that says *Not about to get murdered by Logan Whitmere?* The bar is down the street from here. I had this hope that it could show him in one of his tempers, punching anything that moves, to at least show that he was provoking anyone, but the odds of catching it on tape were low.

Mr. Hawkins pats my hand gently. "I'm sorry

I can't be of more help, dear. Don't you worry, the truth will come out. It always does."

I force a smile, touched by his kindness despite my frustration. "Thanks. You're probably right, but it sure is taking its time."

"You want a wood stain for pine?"

I just close my mouth and give him a small wave of goodbye. I push the door open and step out into the warm autumn air. For a split second, I allow myself to close my eyes and take a deep breath. But when I open them, my momentary peace shatters.

Kyle stands there, flanked by his two lackeys, Randall and Lucas. Their smug grins make my stomach churn.

"Well, well. If it isn't the circus freak's little whore," Kyle sneers, his voice dripping with disdain.

I clench my fists, anger bubbling up inside me. The remnants of Kyle's black eye and split lip from his fight with Logan are still visible, which is a small satisfaction.

"What do you want, Kyle?" I spit out, my voice low and dangerous.

He takes a step closer, his buddies moving to flank me. "Just checking in on our town's newest celebrity. How's your boyfriend enjoying his new accommodations?"

"Fuck off," I growl, trying to push past them.

Randall blocks my path, his meaty hand pressing against my shoulder. "Not so fast, sweetheart. We're not done catching up."

I slap his hand away, my patience wearing thin. "Touch me again, and you'll lose that hand."

Lucas laughs, a harsh, grating sound. "Ooh, she's got claws. I like 'em feisty."

Kyle's eyes narrow, his smirk turning cruel. "You know, Sienna, things would be a lot easier for you if you just admitted the truth. Tell everyone what a violent psychopath your circus freak really is."

"The only psychopath I see is you," I snarl, my anger finally boiling over. "You're the one who kidnapped me, thinking that made you a man. Well, news flash, you're nothing but a small-town bully with daddy issues."

Kyle's face contorts with rage, his hand shooting out to grab my arm. I twist away, my circus training kicking in as I dodge his grasp.

"You little bitch—"

"We all know the real reason you're pushing this case. Logan humiliated you, and now you're using your uncle's position to get revenge."

Kyle's face twists into an ugly sneer. "You

think you're so smart, don't you? Always did have a big mouth."

"At least I use mine for telling the truth. Why don't you man up and admit it? You're only doing this because Logan kicked your ass."

His eyes flash dangerously, and he takes a menacing step forward. "You want to know what I think about that?"

I hold my ground, even as alarm bells start ringing in my head.

Kyle's voice drops to a low, threatening growl. "I'll show you exactly what I think," he snarls, closing the distance between us. His intent is clear in the predatory gleam of his eyes, the way his fists clench at his sides. This isn't just about intimidation anymore. The promise of violence, or worse, hangs heavy in the air.

Asshole #1 and Asshole #2 move to block any potential escape routes, their leers making my skin crawl. They're not just here as backup. They're active participants in whatever Kyle has planned.

"What's wrong, Sienna?" Kyle taunts, his breath hot on my face. "Not so brave without your freak to protect you, are you?"

I swallow hard, fighting to keep my voice steady. "You're not going to get away with this. People will see—"

He cuts me off with a harsh laugh. "See what? A whore getting what she deserves? Trust me, sweetheart. No one's going to lift a finger to help you."

I grit my teeth, my heart pounding like a war drum as Kyle and the assholes tighten their circle around me. The alleyway looms dark and menacing behind them, a stark contrast to the bustling main street we're being shoved away from.

"Get off me!" I snarl, trying to twist out of Asshole #1's grip. His fingers dig into my arm, a cruel vise that makes me wince.

Kyle smirks, his eyes gleaming with malice. "Not so fast, sweetheart. We're just getting started."

I kick out, my boot connecting with Asshole #2's shin. He curses, hopping back briefly before lunging forward again, grabbing at my waist.

"Fucking bitch," he growls, his hands rough and greedy.

Panic surges through me, but I refuse to let it show. I thrash, claw, and bite, fighting with every ounce of strength I have. But they're bigger, stronger, and fueled by a sickening sense of entitlement.

Kyle grabs the front of my shirt, squeezing a breast through the cotton hard enough to bring tears to my eyes. I gasp in pain.

"Bastard!" I claw at Kyle's face, leaving red welts across his cheek.

He curses, backhanding me hard enough to make my ears ring.

My head spins, but I refuse to let them see me falter. I spit blood, aiming for Kyle's smug face. He dodges, laughing.

"You're gonna pay for that," he snarls, reaching for my jeans.

Panic surges through me. I kick and thrash, but the assholes hold me tight. I open my mouth to scream—"What the hell is going on here?"

The booming voice cuts through the alley like a thunderclap. Kyle freezes, his hand still on my belt. We all turn to see Mayor Lindon standing at the alley's entrance, his face a mask of fury.

"Let her go. Now." His voice is low, dangerous.

For a moment, no one moves. Then Kyle's grip loosens, and the assholes step back. I stumble, catching myself against the wall.

Mayor Lindon's eyes sweep over the scene, taking in my disheveled appearance and the boys' guilty faces. "You three, get out of here."

Kyle opens his mouth to argue, but the mayor silences him with a glare.

They slink away, shooting venomous glares at me as they go.

My hands shake as I try to straighten my clothes, avoiding the mayor's gaze. I tug my shirt back into place, wincing at the soreness where Kyle grabbed me.

"Are you alright, Miss Cole?" Mayor Lindon asks, his voice surprisingly gentle. The mayor has always turned a blind eye to the bullshit in this town.

I nod, not meeting his eyes. "I'm fine," I lie.

The mayor takes a step closer, and I tense instinctively. But he just sighs, sounding tired and old. "This shouldn't have happened."

I'm not sure whether he means what happened in this alleyway or the murder case. Or maybe he's talking about entire decades of violence visited upon the Cole women. "Why did you help me?"

Though that's not really what I'm asking.

Why *didn't* you help me?

That's what I really want to know.

If he was capable of stopping Kyle and any other asshole in this town, why wait until this moment to start doing it?

Mayor Lindon sighs, rubbing his forehead. "He's not a good kid. I know that."

I let out a harsh laugh. "Then why hasn't anyone done anything about it?"

"It's complicated. The Moore family… They have a lot of influence in this town. People are afraid."

"So you all just let him terrorize everyone?" My voice rises, anger replacing fear. People are afraid in the circus. They're afraid in Forrester. That fear is like gunpowder. People like Kyle are the match.

"It's not that simple," he says, his shoulders sagging.

I cross my arms, wincing at the soreness. "You're the mayor. I didn't think you signed up for just being the mayor of simple things."

His expression mixes concern and resignation. "Honestly? I think you should leave town, Sienna. Like you tried before. It's not safe for you here."

"I won't abandon him. Not now, not ever."

"You're stubborn, just like your mother."

I stiffen at the mention but push past it. "If you really want to help, do something about Logan. About this whole corrupt system."

He hesitates, and I can see the internal struggle playing out on his face. He shakes his head. "This is out of my hands."

CHAPTER ELEVEN

I CLUTCH MY phone, pacing the length of the circus tent, the vibrant colors dulled by the winter chill. "Professor Stratford, I appreciate your time. I know you're busy."

"Not at all, Miss Cole. I'm intrigued by your vision for a *Romeo and Juliet* performance in a circus setting," William Stratford's voice crackles through the speaker, smooth and authoritative.

I take a deep breath. "We want to emphasize the themes of love, tragedy, and sacrifice. Something powerful that resonates with our audience."

"Of course, those are essential elements," he replies. "However, it's also worth noting that *Romeo and Juliet* can be viewed as a coming-of-age story. The lovers are young, impetuous, and their tragic end underscores their immaturity."

My heart sinks. A coming-of-age story? That's not what I had in mind. "I see," I say, unable to mask my disappointment.

"But wait," he interrupts, a hint of amusement in his tone. "Your point about romance is valid too. Remember, all those fancy analyses and notes in the margins? Shakespeare didn't write them. He wanted his plays to be open to interpretation."

I stop pacing, hope rekindling inside me. "So you mean… there's no single right answer?"

"Precisely," he affirms. "Even so-called experts in Shakespeare disagree on interpretations. Which means there's no single correct answer. There's only how the plays move us."

A smile tugs at my lips. "That's reassuring. We want our show to be something that captures the raw emotion and intensity of their love."

"And it sounds like you're on the right track," Stratford says. "I'm excited to see how you bring this to life under the big top. His plays weren't all serious and tragic. He was a fan of comedy. Of lightness. Of laughter. The circus is a beautiful place to honor one of his works."

I can't help but let out a small laugh of relief. "Thank you, Professor Stratford. Your insights mean a lot to us."

"Send me tickets when you premiere," he says, a smile in his voice. "I'd love to see it in person."

"Absolutely," I promise.

As I hang up, a renewed sense of purpose courses through me. Our *Romeo and Juliet* will be more than just a tale of star-crossed lovers. It will be an emotional journey that captivates our audience's hearts.

The tent is alive with activity—acrobats flipping through the air with breathtaking ease, musicians tuning their instruments to create an atmosphere of enchantment. Every performer moves with a sense of urgency and purpose and incredible skill. Without Nadia, we're not including a trapeze solo. Instead we have two people on silks, both strong athletes who are excited for the show.

The lack of a ringmaster is a little more tricky.

Emerson Durand was an asshole.

But he was a damned good ringmaster.

I'm not sure who can replace him.

It comes to me: we don't have to replace him. What if the story isn't told to us, explained to us, fed to us with the notes in the margin? What if people in the audience can explore the emotions it brings up in them?

What if the show means something a little

different to everyone?

I'm lost in thought, choreographing the next scene in my head, when a familiar yip breaks my concentration. My heart leaps as I spin around to see Maisie standing at the tent entrance, Tricks wriggling excitedly in her arms.

"Surprise!" Maisie grins, setting the little dog down.

Tricks bolts toward me, his tiny paws skittering across the mats on the floor. I drop to my knees, scooping him up as he showers my face with enthusiastic licks.

"Oh, I missed you, buddy," I laugh, burying my face in his soft fur.

Maisie approaches, her blonde curls bouncing with each step. "How's the new show coming?"

I stand, cradling Tricks. "Slow but steady. What's the word on the outside?"

She pulls out her phone, scrolling through a series of articles. "Support for Logan's growing. People are sharing stories about how the circus changed their lives. It's gaining traction."

Hope flutters in my chest. "That's great."

"That's not even the best part," Maisie's eyes sparkle with excitement. "One of our videos went mega-viral! Like it's got a million likes and counting."

My heart races. "Which one? The one about Logan's case?"

"Not exactly. It's that amazing aerial silk routine you guys were practicing yesterday. People are losing their minds over it."

My excitement deflates. "Oh. That's… good, I guess. But it won't help clear Logan's name."

Maisie puts a hand on my arm. "Don't you see? It's all connected. The viral video shows how talented and professional your circus is. It's part of the bigger picture—the story of this amazing group trapped by small-town prejudice."

"You're right," I say, scratching Tricks behind the ears. "It all helps. In a way this has always been more about public opinion than the facts of the case."

Maisie grins. "That's what best friends are for."

We read through some of the comments—most of them enthusiastic, some of them derogatory, because it's the internet.

Wolfgang appears in the practice tent.

His eyes narrow at Maisie. "What the hell are you doing here?"

"More than you," she says without missing a beat.

"I'd say so." It doesn't sound like a compliment. "We got people calling saying they want to get tickets, but they can't. What the hell's that about? Why can't they buy tickets? We can't have sold out."

She snorts, the sound still somehow feminine. "Yeah, because the auctions are going bananas. Tickets are up to two thousand bucks apiece."

My mouth drops open. "Are you serious?"

Wolfgang's usual stoic expression softens almost imperceptibly. "Hell."

Maisie stands a little taller. "Yeah. Hell."

I can't help but smile. There's definitely something brewing there.

The moment is broken by the shrill ring of Maisie's phone. She jumps, fumbling to pull it from her pocket.

"Oh my God," she gasps, staring at the screen. "It's CNN!"

Holy shit. "Answer it!"

Maisie nods, her eyes wide. "I'm going," she says, already heading for the exit. "I'll be back for Tricks later."

As Maisie dashes out, I turn to Wolfgang, an impish grin spreading across my face. "So," I say, drawing out the word, "do you still think Maisie is an enemy townie who doesn't belong here?"

Wolfgang grunts. "Maybe not."

I lower my voice conspiratorially. "Because from where I'm standing, it looked like a certain knife thrower might be having soft and fuzzy feelings."

He crosses his arms over his chest. "She's… spirited."

"Mm-hmm."

"We have bigger things to worry about than my fuzzy feelings."

"Yeah," I say, my smile fading as reality sets back in. "But it's good to see some light in all the darkness."

Tricks is busy charming treats from a group of jugglers. I call him over. His ears perk up at the sound of my voice, and he scampers over.

"Alright, buddy," I say, crouching down to his level. "Time to earn your kibble. Or the oat berry energy bar they were feeding you."

I lead him to the center of the practice area, where the ribbons are set for the death scene. The routine is breathtaking—a fluid, heart-wrenching duet that symbolizes the tragic end of *Romeo and Juliet*. But after such an emotional climax, we need something to lift the audience's spirits.

That's where Tricks comes in.

Except we seem to be missing our Juliet.

"Where's Cat?" I ask Romeo, aka Felix.

He shrugs. "She's been gone a lot."

Shit. That's not like her. Is she still resentful about my role here?

I have to figure out what's happening with her, but not right now.

Now it's practice time.

"Okay, Tricks," I say, holding up his tiny brown robe. "Let's get you into character."

He sits patiently as I slip the costume over his head, adjusting it so his paws are free. With his floppy ear and the oversized robe, he looks absolutely ridiculous—and completely adorable.

"Perfect." I grin. "You're officially Friar Laurence."

I set up a small vial on the other side of the practice area, filled with water dyed a deep purple. "Alright, Friar," I say, pointing to the vial. "Go fetch the poison."

Tricks cocks his head, his eyes darting between me and the vial. I repeat the command, and he takes off, his little robe flapping behind him. He grabs the vial carefully in his mouth and trots back, tail wagging proudly.

"Good boy!"

CHAPTER TWELVE

THAT EVENING, TRICKS is back at the Young household and I'm at home. Maisie has given me online interviews that are straining the ability of our internet. My cellphone rings, and I jump. Shit. Did I forget an interview?

"Hello?"

"It's Sheriff Dunham," he says, his oily voice making me shudder. "Just thought I'd give you a friendly heads-up. That little video stunt of yours? That kind of thing don't matter in Forrester. We're old school."

My fingers tighten around the phone. "Why are you calling me?"

He chuckles, the sound grating on my nerves. "You think a few social media posts are gonna overturn hard evidence? That's cute. But this ain't some TV show where the power of hashtags saves the day."

"People are paying attention, so no more inventing evidence."

"Nice try, sweetheart. Your circus boy is going to prison, and no amount of internet bullshit is gonna change that."

The call ends, leaving me shaking with fury... and fear. I want to scream, to throw my phone across the room, to do something. But I take a deep breath, trying to steady myself as I head downstairs.

The familiar musty smell hits me as my eyes adjust to the dim interior. My mother sits in her usual spot, a chipped teacup cradled in her hands. The curtains are drawn, as always, shutting out the world beyond.

Heavy curtains block out any hint of sunlight, casting everything in a dull, lifeless gray.

"It looks like a prison in here," I mutter, more to myself.

My mother's voice, soft and brittle, catches me off guard. "Anything can be a prison. A room. A thought. And that's what I deserve."

I whip around to face her, confusion etching itself across my face. "What are you saying?"

She doesn't answer, just stares into her teacup as if it holds all the secrets of the universe. "It doesn't matter."

"You know, you don't have to live like this. We could open the curtains, let some light in—"

"No," she cuts me off, her voice sharper than I've heard in years.

With a sigh, I make my way to the kitchen, the floorboards creaking beneath my feet. I pour myself a cup from her kettle and sit across from my mother. The silence stretches between us, thick and heavy. I take a sip of tea, grimacing at the bitter taste. It's been steeping too long, just like everything else in this house.

The irony isn't lost on me. I've spent so much time trying to escape this town, this house, and now here I am, right back where I started.

The walls seem to close in around us, trapping us in this self-made prison of memories and regrets. My mother and I, two generations of women, sitting in the dark, sipping tea that's gone cold.

I set my cup down with a clink.

My mother's gaze shifts from her teacup. "What's wrong, Sienna?"

"All this work might be for nothing. The fake evidence… Logan could be imprisoned for life." My voice wavers, and I hate the vulnerability in it.

She reaches across the table to touch my hand.

"Logan is innocent."

"Mom…"

"Oh, I know he hit your father. Put him in the hospital. But he didn't kill him."

The certainty in her tone startles me. "He died because of his injuries."

She takes a deep breath, eyes closing for a moment as if bracing herself for what she's about to say. "They said he might wake up. I couldn't let that happen."

My heart stutters in my chest. "What are you saying?"

Tears glisten in her eyes. "I unplugged the life support."

The words hang heavy in the air between us, each one like a lead weight dragging me down. I stare at her, trying to process what she just confessed.

"You… you did?" My voice is barely more than a whisper.

She nods slowly, her grip on my hand unyielding. "He was a monster. I couldn't let him come back and hurt us again."

Emotion crashes over me like a tidal wave— relief that Logan didn't kill my father, guilt for ever doubting him, and an overwhelming sadness for my mother's burden.

"Why didn't you tell me?"

She looks down at our joined hands. "I was scared. And ashamed. I thought no one would understand."

Tears spill over my cheeks as I pull her into a hug, holding on to her as if she might disappear. "Mom," I whisper into her hair. "If anyone understands, it's me."

I hold her for a long time. She seems relieved, as if holding back the truth was costing her something. I don't feel relieved, though. I'm torn.

Logan is innocent. The thought should bring comfort, but it doesn't.

Not with the price tag attached.

I sink into my small twin mattress, my heart pounding against my ribs. What do I do with this? Free Logan or protect my mother?

The decision eats at me, each option tearing at the fabric of loyalty.

Logan behind bars because of false accusations, his life slipping away with every passing day. My mother getting the death penalty if her secret gets out.

I need Logan. But at what cost?

I rub my temples, trying to soothe the headache brewing there. Memories of Patrick's cruelty flicker through my mind—his fists, his venomous words—but also the rare moments of tenderness that made staying feel like an obligation.

Does he deserve justice? Or does my mother deserve peace?

The truth slices through the fog of confusion and anger that's clouded my mind for so long. My mother isn't just a victim; she's also a savior in her own right. The law won't see her that way, but I do.

I sit on the edge of my old bed, the faded quilt rough beneath my fingers. The room smells like dust and forgotten dreams. Posters of pop stars from another era cling to the walls, their colors muted by time. I reach for a box under the bed, pulling it out with a cloud of dust that makes me cough.

Inside, a jumble of childhood relics greets me. I sift through them, finding a stuffed bear missing an eye, a broken music box that once played "Twinkle, Twinkle, Little Star," and finally, a single photo that stops me cold.

Maisie and I grin at the camera, our mouths stained blue from snow cones. Her parents had taken us to the county fair. I remember the thrill of the rides, the laughter that bubbled up from somewhere deep inside me, so rare in my childhood. My parents hadn't taken me to the fair. My father had been off somewhere getting drunk and picking fights while my mother had stayed home, sipping tea in this very house.

I trace Maisie's face with my finger. We look so happy, so innocent. The photo mocks me now—a snapshot of joy in a life filled with shadows.

My childhood was a sad one, punctuated by moments of fear and loneliness. Now I understand why my mother thinks she deserves prison.

She thinks she's atoning for her sins.

Except there were no sins.

My father was an evil man who didn't deserve to live. He had taken so much from us—our peace, our happiness, our freedom. My mother did what she had to do to end his reign of terror.

I won't let her continue to suffer for his actions.

The decision settles over me like a shroud, heavy but resolute. I can't betray my mother by revealing her secret. Logan will have to stay locked up for now, an innocent man caught in the web of small-town prejudice.

As I drift off, the world around me shifts and blurs. Suddenly, I'm sitting in a courtroom, but everything tilts off-kilter. The walls seem to bend at impossible angles, and the floor beneath my feet undulates like waves.

I look down and realize I'm sitting at the defense table, dressed in a suit that doesn't quite fit right. Across the aisle, my mother stands tall and imposing, her usually meek demeanor replaced by a fierce determination. She's the prosecuting attorney, her eyes blazing with an intensity I've never seen before.

The judge's bench looms before us, and my stomach drops when I see Kyle sitting there, a smug grin plastered across his face. He's wearing the judge's robes, but they hang off him awkwardly, like a child playing dress-up.

"Order in the court," Kyle drawls, his voice echoing unnaturally in the warped space.

I turn to look at the defendant's chair, and my heart nearly stops. Logan sits there, his hands cuffed, his eyes fixed on me with a mixture of confusion and betrayal.

The trial proceeds in a blur of nonsensical arguments and twisted logic. My mother presents evidence that makes no sense—a broken teacup, a faded circus poster, my old stuffed bear. I try to object, but my voice comes out as a whisper.

Finally, Kyle bangs his gavel, the sound reverberating through my skull. "I've heard enough," he announces. "What's the verdict?"

The jury box is empty, but a chorus of voices fills the air. "Guilty," they chant, over and over.

"Guilty," Kyle echoes, a triumphant gleam in his eye.

I turn to Logan, desperate to explain, to apologize, but the words die in my throat. His face contorts with fury, eyes burning into mine.

"You are the cause of this," he snarls, his voice dripping with venom. "You betrayed me, Sienna. You're no better than the rest of them."

I jolt awake, heart pounding, sweat beading on my forehead. The dream clings to me like a second skin, leaving me shaken and disoriented.

I wake with a start, my eyes gritty and heavy. Weak morning light filters through the broken blinds, casting thin stripes across my childhood bedroom. For a moment, I'm disoriented, caught between the lingering tendrils of my nightmare and the harsh reality of waking up in this place again.

My phone buzzes insistently on the nightstand, jarring me fully awake. I fumble for it, squinting at the screen. Not the sheriff again, thank God.

"Hello?" My voice is husky with sleep.

"I've got something you're gonna want to see." Cat's voice crackles with excitement.

I sit up, suddenly alert. "What is it?"

She pauses, and I can almost hear her grin through the phone. "I've got proof. Proof of the sheriff's unethical efforts to cover for Kyle."

My heart races. "How?"

"Let's just say I've been… getting close to the sheriff. Seducing him, actually." There's a hint of pride in her voice. "And now I've got recordings. Conversations that'll prove he's a lying sack of shit."

I'm speechless for a moment, torn between hope and horror. "Cat, that's… that's incredible. But also incredibly dangerous. Are you okay?"

She laughs, a sound that's both bitter and triumphant. "I'm fine. Better than fine. I'm bringing that bastard down. You were right, you know? What you said in the tent. He did so much for me. This was the least I could do."

She seduced him… I want to believe that she started to but didn't have to go through with it? That seems unlikely. I'm afraid to ask. I feel a mix of gratitude and guilt. Cat endangered herself, all to help Logan. It makes me sad, but I also can't wish for anything different. Not if it means Logan going free.

CHAPTER THIRTEEN

I PACE BACK and forth outside the jail, the hot morning air dampening my skin. My heart pounds in my chest. It took three long days of bullshit to get the judge back in session so we could present the new evidence. With the proof of the sheriff's corruption, it cast everything he said about Logan into doubt. The case was dismissed an hour ago.

Tricks whines softly at my feet, sensing my anxiety. I glance at the imposing building, its brick walls holding Logan captive, and a knot of dread tightens in my stomach.

Every minute lasts an eternity.

I try to focus on the rhythmic sound of my footsteps against the cracked pavement, but it does little to calm my nerves.

Finally, the heavy door creaks open, and Logan steps out. He looks rumpled and slightly filthy, his clothes disheveled from his time inside. His eyes are haunted, shadows lingering in their depths.

The sight of him makes my breath catch in my throat.

I rush to him, wrapping my arms around his broad shoulders in a tight embrace. Relief floods through me as I feel his solid form against mine.

He's free.

He squeezes me back, but there's a hesitance in his touch. His arms encircle me like they always have, but something is different now.

"I'm so glad you're out," I whisper.

"Yeah," he mutters, his voice low and rough-edged.

When I pull back to look at him, he doesn't quite meet my eyes.

I step back to study his face more closely. The haunted look in his eyes sends a shiver down my spine. Jail has left its mark on him in ways that even sunlight can't dispel.

"Are you okay?" My voice trembles despite my effort to keep it steady.

He gives a half-hearted nod. "Of course."

Tricks barks and nuzzles against Logan's leg, offering a small distraction from the tension between us. Logan kneels down to pet him, and for a moment, some of the darkness lifts from his eyes.

"We should get you home," I say softly.

Logan stands up slowly, brushing off some of the dirt from his pants. "Home," he says, a weariness in his tone that wasn't there before. "Not sure I have one of those."

A sleek, dark armored SUV pulls up beside us. The tinted windows and imposing presence make my heart skip a beat. I recognize the North Security logo on the side and turn to Logan.

"What do you mean?" I ask, my voice wavering.

Logan's jaw tightens. "I'm not going back to the circus."

My brow furrows. "Right now?"

"Ever."

"But you have to."

His face darkens, shadows creeping across his features. The haunted look in his eyes intensifies, and I feel a chill run down my spine.

"I'm done with Cirque des Miroirs," he says, his voice low and gravelly. "It's from a different part of my life. I don't need it anymore."

I stare at him, stunned. The circus is his life, his passion. How can he just walk away from it all?

"You can't mean that," I whisper, reaching for his hand.

He pulls away, and the gesture cuts deep. "I do mean it. Being in that cell brought back everything I've tried to forget. I can't go back."

I feel like the ground is shifting beneath my feet. Everything we've built, everything we've fought for... It's over? "But what about the performers, the crew... They need you."

Logan's eyes flash with a mix of pain and anger. "They'll be fine without me. You've been running things while I was locked up, haven't you?"

His words feel like a slap in the face.

"Shit," he mutters. "I didn't mean it like that."

My heart breaks in that moment. Logan stands right in front of me, but he might as well be across the galaxy. The weight of his pain is palpable, hanging heavy in the air between us.

I take a step back, my legs shaking beneath me. "Logan," I whisper, my voice quivering. "I... I love you. You know that, right?"

His eyes meet mine, and for a moment, I see a flicker of the man I fell in love with. But it's quickly overshadowed by the darkness that's consumed him.

"I know," he says softly.

I swallow hard, fighting back tears. "Whatever you need to do, wherever you need to go… I'll support you. No matter what. If you want to go to North Security, I'll go with you."

The words taste bitter on my tongue. Every fiber of my being wants to beg him to reconsider, but that's not what he needs right now.

Logan's gaze doesn't quite meet mine. "Thank you," he says, his voice a mix of relief and sorrow. "For understanding. For everything."

I nod, not trusting myself to speak.

Tricks whines at my feet, sensing the tension in the air.

I climb into the SUV beside Logan, my heart heavy with uncertainty. The leather seats are cool against my skin, a stark contrast to the warmth I'd imagined for our reunion. Tricks settles at my feet, his small body pressed against my leg as if sensing my need for comfort.

The SUV pulls onto the road, and I steal a glance at Logan. His jaw is set, eyes fixed on the road ahead. The man beside me is a stranger, worlds away from the passionate, driven circus owner I fell in love with.

"So, North Security," I say, trying to keep my

voice light. "Alex Harrison. Cirque des Miroirs has an impressive lineup of professionals protecting it."

Logan's response is curt. "We have a lot of enemies."

I nod, swallowing hard. Enemies I brought them. "Right."

Silence falls between us again.

My mind races, replaying the last few weeks. All the work we've put into the circus, the new *Romeo and Juliet* show, keeping everyone together. It was all for him. I thought when he got out, he'd be proud, excited to see what we've accomplished.

"Logan," I start, my voice barely above a whisper. "About the show—"

"I told you, Sienna," he cuts me off, his tone sharp. "I'm done with it."

"Everyone's been working so hard on the new show."

He turns to me, his eyes blazing. "Did I ask you to do that?"

I shrink back, stunned by the venom in his voice. "No, but—"

"Then leave it the hell alone," he says, turning back to the window.

His words cut deep, and I feel tears pricking at my eyes. I blink them back, determined not to let him see how much he's hurting me.

As we drive through Forrester, I watch the familiar streets pass by. The town that once felt like a prison now seems almost welcoming compared to the cold silence in this car.

I try to tell myself it's just the shock of his release. That he needs time to adjust, to process everything that's happened. But a nagging voice in the back of my mind whispers that this is something more, something permanent.

CHAPTER FOURTEEN

"TECHNICALLY, THERE'S STILL some risk the case could be brought again," the tinny voice says through the speaker. Logan listens with a stoic intensity. My stomach clenches. After everything, could they really drag Logan back into this nightmare?

The lawyer's still at the courthouse, firming things up.

And apparently, the receptionist was Harrison's inside source at the sheriff's office. She also still hates me. It's possible to snitch on someone for being a dirty cop while still believing their sexist lies. She's proof of that.

"That's unlikely," Harrison continues. "It would only reveal that the acting sheriff is equally tainted with corruption. So most likely, you're safe now, Logan. I want you to remain completely above suspicion. When you leave the area, make your whereabouts clear."

Logan nods. "Fine."

"Then again, that won't be hard," the lawyer says, "with the media coverage."

Dark green eyes narrow. "The what?"

Um. Time to fess up. "I asked Maisie to start some social media accounts for the circus. To showcase our side of the story with your case."

A rough sigh. "Hell. It's the performers' job to be in the spotlight, not mine."

"Well, we also used it to promote the new show."

"That's good," he says in a voice that sounds like the opposite.

"It's drummed up tons of interest—we've got a whole new legion of fans dying to see us perform once we announce the new tour schedule."

"I know I should be grateful. I *am* grateful."

"You're just a private person."

"Right."

"And you're stuck in the 1960s with all this vintage circus shit."

He huffs a laugh. "Yeah, okay."

"This is a good thing," I tell him, trying to sound hopeful.

"I believe you."

Emboldened by his words, by the fact that we're together and free again at last, I lean in to kiss him. Logan turns his face away at the last second, causing my lips to land awkwardly on his stubbled cheek instead.

Shame rises inside me. "What's wrong?"

"Nothing, I just…" He runs a hand over his tired face, looking pained. "I feel disgusting. I was in that grimy cell for weeks. I haven't had a real shower. I don't want to get you dirty."

My heart clenches at the anguish in his voice, the self-loathing.

He's always been so strong, so solid—my unshakable foundation in the chaotic whirlwind of circus life. To see him brought this low, doubting himself, breaks something in me. It's not about the physical dirt of that place, even if there is a distinct… odor.

It's about the memories it brought up in him.

I'm not sure they're going to be shoved back down.

"You could never dirty me," I say. "Not ever."

Logan is already turning away, his broad shoulders tense. "I'm going to grab a shower," he mutters, tossing his phone onto the bed.

I watch him go, listening to the sound of the

bathroom door clicking shut, then the hiss of the shower spray coming to life. The rushing water echoes the furious pounding of my pulse.

I know I should probably give him space, let him wash away the grime and degradation of his incarceration in peace.

Anything can be a prison.

That's what my mother said.

Is that what the shower is for Logan right now?

Not a place of cleansing and renewal, but another kind of prison?

I'm moving before I even consciously decide to, my feet carrying me across the plush carpet to the bathroom door. I pause for only a second, my hand on the knob, my heart in my throat. Then, reckless, desperate, I step inside.

Humidity hits me like a wall, the air thick and heavy with steam. Through the foggy glass of the shower door, I can just make out Logan's muscled form. He's standing motionless under the spray, his head bowed, body tensed as if he's bracing for a blow.

He looks lost. Alone.

Utterly defeated, in a way I've never seen him, in a way that scares me far more than any of the dangers I've faced in Forrester.

I have to go to him. Have to show him that he's not alone, that he hasn't lost himself or my love. That he never could.

Quietly, I shed my clothes, leaving them in a crumpled heap on the tile. Then I pad toward the shower, reach for the door handle, and step into the scalding spray.

The water is painfully hot against my skin as I slip into the shower behind Logan, but I can't worry about that. All of my attention is focused on the slope of his broad shoulders, the corded muscles of his back, the way his whole body seems to be vibrating with a tension that's almost palpable.

Slowly, carefully, I reach out and press my palm between his shoulder blades. He flinches at the contact but doesn't pull away. Emboldened, I step closer, molding my body to his, my breasts against his back, my cheek resting on his slick skin.

"I'm here," I whisper, my voice barely audible over the pounding of the water. "And I'm not going anywhere. You're not alone."

For a long moment, he doesn't respond.

Then, with a shuddering sigh that seems to come from the depths of his soul, he turns to face me. His eyes, when they meet mine, are hooded and haunted, filled with a pain that takes my breath away.

"This is hell," he rasps, his voice rough with emotion.

"Shh," I soothe, bringing my hands up to frame his face. "It's okay. You don't have to have it figured out right now. Just let me take care of you."

And slowly, reverently, I begin to do just that. I reach for the soap and work up a lather in my hands, then smooth them over his chest, his arms, his stomach. I wash away the grime and the sweat, the invisible scars of his time behind bars.

More than that, I try to pour all of my love, all of my fierce, unshakable devotion, into every touch. I want him to feel it seeping into his skin, soaking into his bones. I want him to know, beyond any doubt, that he is cherished.

That he is worth fighting for.

"I love you," I murmur as I slide my soapy hands over the planes of his back. "I love you, Logan. No matter what."

He makes a broken sound, somewhere between a sob and a growl, and suddenly his arms are around me, crushing me to him. His mouth finds mine in a desperate, bruising kiss that steals the breath from my lungs.

"Sienna," he groans against my lips. "My sunset."

Despite the tenderness of the moment, I can feel the tension coiled in Logan's body. The memory of his confinement lingers, his father's presence like a third person in the shower, a ghostly malevolence.

I reach down to touch him, to grasp his hard cock.

He flinches, as if my touch burns. "No," he rasps. "Don't."

Pain lurches inside me. I feel his humiliation as if it's my own. But I also know that healing doesn't come from running away or hiding. It comes from facing the darkness head-on, together.

"You said you would wait until you were free. Well, you're free now, Logan. We're both free. I want you. Your body. Your climax. Your cum."

He looks at me with haunted eyes, desire simmering beneath the surface. The need to reclaim what was taken from him. "I don't have any control left. I'll be too rough. And hurt you."

I sink to my knees before him, the water cascading over my shoulders.

I take him in my mouth, savoring the taste of him, salty and musky and uniquely Logan. His cock is hard and heavy on my tongue, a testament to his desire despite the lingering shadows in his eyes. I can feel the tension in his body, the way he's holding himself back, trying not to lose control.

I want him to lose control. I want him to let go of the fear and the pain and just be in this moment with me. So I suck harder, swirling my tongue around the head of his cock, teasing the sensitive spot just beneath.

Be rough, I tell him with every swipe of my tongue. *Hurt me.*

I would relish that pain.

It means he's free. He's alive. He's safe.

He groans, his fingers tightening in my hair as he pushes deeper into my mouth. I relax my throat, taking him as far as I can. His cock hits the back of my throat. The water from the shower is hot and misty around us, beading on my skin and running down my back in rivulets, a thousand tiny kisses, heightening every sensation.

Logan's hips start to move, thrusting gently in and out of my mouth. His muscles turn hard, tension building in him, his whole body coiled like a spring. I reach up to cup his balls, rolling them gently in my hand as I suck harder.

He groans again, louder this time, and I can feel his cock swell in my mouth. He's close, so close, and I want to be the one to push him over the edge. I redouble my efforts, sucking and licking and teasing until he's panting and trembling above me.

And then, with a final, guttural groan, he comes. His cock pulses in my mouth, hot and salty, and I swallow every drop, savoring the taste of him. He sags against the shower wall, his breath coming in ragged gasps, and I look up at him with a satisfied smile.

"Fuck, Sunset," he gasps, his voice hoarse. "I don't deserve you."

I stand up, pressing my body against his. His heart pounds against my chest. "I love you," I whisper, my lips brushing against his ear.

He turns his head, capturing my mouth in a searing kiss. "Thank you," he murmurs, his hands sliding down to cup my ass. "For everything."

We spend far too long in the shower. Unlike the water heater at home, this one never seems to run out. We're there for over an hour. He makes use of the time, running his hands over my body, soaping my breasts, my stomach, the place between my legs. I gasp when he slides two fingers inside me. I'm still hot from sucking his cock, and he keeps me on that knife-edge of arousal, using his hands, his mouth, and the spray of water.

Logan's hands are everywhere, touching and teasing me until I'm a writhing mess under the hot spray of the shower. His fingers slide over my breasts, pinching my nipples until I gasp, then trail down my stomach to the apex of my thighs. He presses his thumb against my clit, rubbing slow circles that make my legs tremble.

"Please," I moan, my voice echoing off the tile walls.

He chuckles darkly, his breath hot against my ear. "Please what, Sunset? Ask nicely if you want to be fucked. Say the words."

"I need you," I beg, my hips bucking against his hand. "I need you inside me. Please fuck me."

He groans, his fingers sliding lower to tease my entrance. "You're so tight," he murmurs, his voice low and rough. "I'm going to stretch you out tonight."

I whimper, my nails digging into his shoulders as he pushes two fingers inside me. He curls them, hitting that spot that makes my vision go white, and I cry out, my head falling back.

"It hurts," I beg again, my voice hoarse.

He growls, his teeth nipping at my earlobe. "You want my cock?"

"Yes," I gasp, my hips rocking against his hand.

He pulls his fingers out of me, and I whimper at the loss. But then he's turning me around, pressing my hands against the shower wall. His cock nudges my entrance, and I push back, desperate to have him inside me.

He groans, his hands gripping my hips as he slides into me inch by inch. I cry out, my body stretching to accommodate him. He's so big, so thick, and—goddamn, *so good.*

He starts to move, his hips thrusting slowly at first, then faster and harder. The water sprays down on us, hot and steamy, as we move together. I can hear the sounds of our moans bouncing off the tile, echoing through the bathroom.

"Oh God," I gasp, my fingers curling against the shower wall.

He groans, his hand reaching around to find my clit. He rubs it in time with his thrusts, and I spiral higher and higher.

"Come for me, Sunset," he growls, his voice low and rough. "Come all over my cock. I want to feel you squeezing me, milking me, making me forget."

I cry out, my body shuddering as I come. He groans, his hips thrusting harder and faster as he follows me over the edge. We're panting and trembling, water washing over us.

"I love you," I whisper, my head falling back against his shoulder.

He presses a kiss to my neck, his arms wrapping around me.

We stand there for a moment, lost in each other, the water cascading around us. And for the first time in weeks, it seems like everything might be okay.

As long as I can ignore the fact that he doesn't say *I love you* anymore.

CHAPTER FIFTEEN

I WAKE UP in North Security headquarters, my body still humming with the aftermath of last night. The early morning light filters through the blinds, casting soft, golden stripes across the room. I'm alone in the room.

My mind swirls with memories of his release from jail, the way he looked at me with such raw vulnerability. The way he claimed me under the hot spray of the shower, like a man starved for touch, for connection.

I reach down and gently stroke Tricks's fur as he lies curled up at my feet. He gives a contented sigh and snuggles closer. My loyal little companion has been through so much with me. I can't help but smile as I think about all the tricks we've practiced together for our new show.

I slip out of bed and pull on my clothes quickly.

Urgency thrums through me.

I have him in body.

I need him in spirit, too.

Tricks stirs and yawns, looking up at me with those big, trusting eyes. "Stay here, buddy," I whisper, giving him a quick scratch behind the ears before heading downstairs.

The house is quiet, the only sounds coming from the soft slap of my feet on the cool marble floors.

Logan stands on a large balcony, framed by the sunlight. He stares at the horizon, lost in thought. The sight of him takes my breath away—so strong yet so vulnerable.

I take a deep breath and walk toward him, my heart pounding in my chest. "Hey," I say softly, my voice barely above a whisper.

He doesn't turn around immediately but his shoulders tense. "Hey," he finally says, his voice rough.

I step closer until I'm standing beside him. The view from here is breathtaking—rolling hills and distant mountains bathed in sunlight—but all I can focus on is Logan.

We're down to *heys* because they're the only words that seem safe. Everything else is sharp, dangerous.

Words like *circus* and *home* and *love*.

I take another deep breath, summoning all my courage. "I know you don't want me to talk about this, but the debut for the show is tomorrow. You deserve to see it. And they deserve to have you there."

He shakes his head, looking away again. "I'm done with that life."

"The circus needs you. And I think you might need the circus."

Something dark flashes across his handsome face. "Because I'm a freak?"

My voice trembles despite my best efforts to keep it steady. "Am I a freak? Is Travis? That's some bullshit. They got into your head."

"They were always in my head," he says quietly. "I was born with them in my head. That's how I was made, Sienna. With cruelty. With rape. And what did I do? I went looking for it. I wanted it."

I grip his arm tighter, forcing him to meet my gaze. "And what about everything you've gained? The family you've built? The community that depends on you?"

He looks at me for a long moment, conflict raging in his eyes.

"You've built something incredible—a family,

a home for so many people. It's a beautiful thing. Something to be proud of."

He rubs his face, eyes weary. "I set up tents, Sienna. Sold popcorn."

"You've given us all a place to belong. You helped me when I had nowhere else to go. That's not something just anyone can do."

He looks down at his hands, clenched tightly on the balcony rail. "And I fucked you. Did you think about that? Would I still have helped you if I didn't want to suck on your tits? If I wasn't already imagining how your cunt would feel around my cock?"

The crude words hit me like a blow, which is how he meant them. "Yes," I say, my voice shaking. "You would have still helped me no matter what."

He finally meets my eyes, pain like white water rapids. "I'm glad you believe that. I know the truth. Which is that you're just a good fuck."

I flinch. "Stop it."

"Stop what?"

"You're being such a bastard, but then, you know that. Would I still have run away with the circus if you hadn't had green eyes and hard abs? Yes, we have sex. Yes, we like it, but that's not all we are. We're safety. We're *home*."

My voice trembles, but I can't stop now. "I've spent my whole life an outsider. Forrester never felt like home. Not once. It was a prison. The only place I ever belonged was the circus. With you."

His eyes flicker with something—pain, maybe regret. "Look how well that turned out. You're right back where you started."

"I used to think that if I could just be strong enough, tough enough, then maybe I could make it on my own. But the truth is, Logan, I'm terrified. Terrified of losing you, terrified of going back to that emptiness." My voice cracks, and I swallow hard against the lump in my throat. "Because I'm not back where I started, as long as you're standing by my side."

His hands grip the railing so tightly his knuckles turn white. He looks out at the horizon as if searching for answers in the distance. "I want to stand by your side, but I'm not sure I'm standing at all. I'm down. Way, way down."

"No," I whisper.

He turns to me then, his eyes filled with a storm of emotions—fear, longing, love. "I don't want to drag you down with me."

"You won't," I promise.

Logan's lips crash against mine, and for a

moment, the world fades away. The kiss is desperate, filled with all the emotions we've been struggling to express. I melt into him, my body responding instinctively to his touch.

As the kiss deepens, becoming more heated and sensual, desire ignites within me. But a small voice in the back of my mind reminds me of the conversation we were having, the importance of what we need to resolve.

Reluctantly, I start to pull away, my breath coming in short gasps. "Logan, wait," I murmur against his lips. "We need to—"

Suddenly, his demeanor changes. His grip on my arms tightens, and his eyes flash with a mixture of pain and anger. "If you're not going to fuck me, then leave me alone," he growls, his voice rough and cold.

I take a step back, shock rippling through me. My mind reels, trying to process this sudden shift. I can see the hurt behind his eyes, the way he's pushing me away to protect himself from more pain. But the harshness of his words, the callousness of his tone, cuts deep.

My heart aches for him, for us, but a surge of self-respect rises within me. I won't let anyone treat me this way, not even Logan. Not even to prove my love.

"I understand you're hurting," I say, my voice trembling but firm. "But I won't let you push me away like this. I care about you too much to watch you self-destruct."

I take another step back, creating more distance between us. "When you're ready to talk—really talk—I'll be here. But I won't be your emotional punching bag, Logan. I deserve better than that, and deep down, you know it too."

He glares at me and then turns to walk away.

The Texas hill country stretches out before me, a patchwork of rolling hills and wildflowers. It's so different from the flat, dusty plains of Forrester where I grew up. Here, the land breathes, the horizon seems to promise something new with each dawn.

I close my eyes, letting the memory of my old tree house wash over me. I can still remember the rough bark under my fingers, hear the creak of the wooden planks as I climbed up to my secret haven. Lying on my back, I'd watch the sunlight filter through the leaves, creating a mosaic of light and shadow. It was in that sanctuary that Maisie had found me one afternoon, breathless and excited.

"The circus is coming to town!" she'd shouted up at me. Her blonde hair glowed in the dappled light as she beamed up at me. That was the day everything changed.

Back then, running away with the circus felt like an escape. A way to break free from a town that never accepted me and a father who made home feel like a prison. But now? Now, I crave the circus for entirely different reasons.

I want it back not as a means of escape but as a place to belong. As home.

But can I really do it without Logan?

I stay on the balcony, my thoughts a tangled mess of memories and hopes. The distant sound of a car engine purring to life pulls me from my reverie. My heart leaps in my chest. Could it be Logan? Has he decided to come back and face everything with me?

I turn quickly, eyes wide with anticipation. But instead of Logan's familiar figure, I see Liam North standing there. His presence is commanding, almost predatory, his lean muscles coiled like a panther ready to strike.

Both men are tall and handsome, but where Liam is a smooth, sharply honed blade, Logan is a serrated knife—brutal and raw.

"Morning," he says, his voice smooth but edged with steel.

"Morning," I reply, trying to mask my disappointment. It's not Logan.

Liam's eyes flicker with understanding as he takes in my expression. "He's upset."

"Yeah," I admit, my shoulders sagging slightly.

He steps closer, his gaze steady and assessing. "He's been through hell. Give him time."

I swallow hard, fighting back the sting of tears. "What if that doesn't work?"

"I see the way he looks at you. If you can be his anchor, he will be okay."

I look at Liam, searching for any sign that he might be right. His confidence is unwavering, but I'm not convinced.

"He said he's done with the circus," I say quietly, more to myself than to Liam.

"People say things when they're hurting," Liam responds. "Doesn't mean they believe it deep down."

I want to believe him, but the doubt gnaws at me. "What if he doesn't come back? What if he can't?"

Liam's expression softens just a fraction. "Then you'll find a way to keep going. You're stronger than you think, Sienna."

His words are meant to comfort, but they only add to the weight on my shoulders. I've always had to be strong—strong for myself, for my mother, for the circus. But right now, all I want is Logan by my side.

"Thanks," I murmur, forcing a small smile.

Liam nods and gives me one last look before heading inside, leaving me alone with my thoughts once more.

The sun continues its climb in the sky, casting long shadows across the landscape.

CHAPTER SIXTEEN

T HAT NIGHT I dream about Logan, but even though he's freed in real life, he's still in jail in my dreams. I see him behind bars. They're getting stronger, even as the world encased in them falls apart. Logan looks rough.

In the dream, Logan's cell morphs into a twisted mockery of reality.

The once-simple iron bars have transformed into thick, corroded prison gates covered with ivy. They're slick with mildew, giving off a sickening stench. Logan's face is gaunt, hollowed out by shadows that cling to his sharp cheekbones. His eyes are sunken, dark circles framing the haunted look that's settled there. He looks like a ghost of himself, trapped in a nightmare that refuses to end.

I watch in horror as the guards drag him from

the cell, their grips cruel and unyielding. They shove him into an old-fashioned electric chair, its leather straps cracked and frayed with age. The sight of it sends a shiver down my spine. Logan's muscular frame looks out of place, almost too large for the ancient contraption meant to deliver death.

"Logan!" I scream.

My voice sounds muted, like I'm shouting through water. He doesn't respond, his gaze fixed on some distant point, as if he's already accepted his fate.

The room around us flickers and warps. Shadows elongate and twist into mocking figures of circus clowns with cruel grins plastered on their faces. Among them stands the specter of his father, tattooed skin stretching grotesquely over muscle and bone. The crowd jeers and laughs, just like they did when his father was paraded as a freak show attraction.

Logan's face contorts in pain—not from the straps digging into his flesh—but from the weight of this twisted legacy bearing down on him. The switch is thrown by one of the clowns, electricity crackling ominously in the air. Logan's body jolts violently as the current courses through him, but it's not just physical agony I see; it's the torment of being unable to escape his past.

His father's face leers at him from the crowd, a vile reminder of everything Logan fears becoming. The mocking laughter crescendos around us, drowning out my desperate cries.

Logan's eyes lock on to mine for a brief moment—filled with sorrow and resignation—before they roll back under his lids. The smell of burned flesh mingles with the mildew, creating a nauseating cocktail that fills my lungs and makes me want to retch.

The dream swirls into chaos as I reach out toward him, my fingers barely brushing against his before he fades away completely, leaving me alone in this hellish circus of nightmares.

My heart pounds against my ribs like it's trying to escape. Sweat clings to my skin, the sheets damp and suffocating. It was a dream. It had to be a dream.

But the bed beside me is empty.

For a split second, panic floods my veins. My mind races back to the jail, the rusty bars, the electric chair. What if it wasn't just a nightmare? What if he's still there, still trapped in that hell? My fingers dig into the mattress, searching for any trace of him, any warmth left behind.

Nothing.

I swing my legs over the edge of the bed, my feet hitting the cold floor with a muted thud. The room is dimly lit by the first light of dawn seeping through the curtains. I'm caught in some cruel limbo between dream and reality.

"Logan?" My voice comes out hoarse, barely more than a whisper. I listen for any sound that might indicate he's here, that he's safe. The house remains silent.

My chest tightens as I remember his hollow eyes, his gaunt face from my dream. The fear that maybe he's still behind bars grips me with icy fingers. Could it all have been a cruel trick of my mind? Him being released, our night together—it felt so real.

My heart still races from the nightmare. The room is dark, shadows stretching long and eerie in the pale moonlight. As I blink away the remnants of sleep, I realize I'm not alone.

Logan sits in the corner, his silhouette rigid and unmoving. Relief washes over me, a tidal wave that crashes hard and fast. He's safe. Not the tortured version from my dream. But something's off. Heavy air suffocates me.

"Logan?" My voice is a whisper, barely cutting through the thick silence.

He doesn't respond immediately, just stares at

the floor. Even in the dim light, I can see he's fully dressed. My eyes adjust further, and that's when I see it—a shadow beside him.

A suitcase.

My breath catches in my throat. It can't be. But there it is, unmistakable and cruelly definitive. Panic flares in my chest, mingling with disbelief.

"You're leaving?" The words spill out before I can stop them.

Logan finally looks up, his eyes meeting mine. There's a sadness there, a resignation that mirrors what I'd seen in my nightmare. He doesn't need to say it; I already know what it means.

He's leaving me.

"No," I choke out, shaking my head as if that could change reality. "You can't."

He runs a hand through his tousled hair, and for a moment, he looks as weary as he did in my dream—trapped by invisible bars only he can see.

"Sienna," he starts, his voice rough and laden with emotion.

Tears well up. I force them back down. This isn't happening. It can't be happening.

"Why?" My voice cracks on the single word.

He sighs deeply, shoulders sagging under an invisible weight. "It's for the best," he says quietly, but there's no conviction in his tone—just an echo of defeat.

I scramble out of bed, crossing the room to stand before him. My hands shake as they reach out to touch his face, to make sure he's real and not another figment of my dreams.

"Don't do this," I plead softly.

He closes his eyes briefly at my touch, as if savoring this last moment before pulling away entirely.

"I'm sorry," he murmurs, opening his eyes to meet mine once more.

His gaze holds a mixture of sorrow and resolve that cuts deeper than any knife ever could.

I kneel down in front of Logan, my knees pressing into the cold, hard floor. The moonlight casts an ethereal glow over us, turning the room into a world where shadows and light dance together in a macabre ballet. His eyes, those deep pools of torment, fixate on me with sorrow.

"I've become my father," he whispers, his voice breaking the fragile silence.

My heart clenches at his words. "Logan, no—"

"I was always him. It's the only explanation for why I joined the circus, why I got these tattoos." His fingers trace the ink on his arms, each line a reminder of the life he's led. "Part of me wanted to pretend, but he was always inside me."

The weight of his self-loathing crashes over me like a tidal wave. I can see the conviction in his eyes, the belief that he's nothing more than a reflection of his father's failures. The assured, confident man who once protected me from bullies before he even knew my name is gone, replaced by this shadow of despair.

"You're not your father," I say firmly, my hands reaching up to cup his face.

He pulls away from my touch as if it burns him. "Don't touch me," he insists, voice thick with emotion. "I tried to escape it, Sienna. I thought my circus would be different—thought it could be something beautiful. But it's just another prison."

His words cut deep, each one a dagger to my heart. I want to shake him, to make him see that he's more than this darkness that's consuming him. But I know it's useless. I can see it in his eyes. He's unreachable.

Tears blur my vision as I search for something—anything—to hold him.

The Logan who saved me from my own hell is slipping away, has already gone, lost in a sea of self-doubt and regret. And no matter how much I want to save him now, I can't fight the ghosts that haunt him.

"Please," I whisper one last time, hoping against hope that something will reach him.

He shakes his head.

Then he's standing, walking away, heading for the door. Leaving my life. My vision blurs with tears, each drop scalding my cheeks as it falls. Good, I don't want to see this happen. I don't want it to be real.

He pauses at the doorway, his back to me. The silence between us stretches, a chasm too wide to cross.

"If you're your father," I manage to choke out, my voice barely above a whisper. "Am I doomed to follow in my mother's footsteps too?"

He turns slowly, his eyes meeting mine with a look that punches me in the gut. There's no warmth there, just a resigned sadness. "Yes," he says quietly, each word a nail in the coffin of my hope. "It's your curse to love a man who will hurt you."

The finality of his statement crushes me. My legs give out and I collapse to the floor, sobs shaking my body. Logan doesn't offer any comfort or solace. He stands there for a moment longer before stepping through the doorway.

His footsteps echo down the hall, each one fainter than the last. They fade far too fast, leaving me alone with nothing but the sound of my own ragged breathing.

I curl into myself on the cold floor, tears streaming down my face. The emptiness he left behind threatens to swallow me whole. Despair wraps around me like a suffocating blanket, heavy and unyielding.

He's gone. Truly gone.

I'm utterly alone.

The show is supposed to be tonight. Except the circus was his dream, his sanctuary. What does it even matter now? Part of me wants to give up, to let everything crumble.

A soft whimper breaks through my fog of misery.

Tricks, with his one ear up and one ear flopped down, trots over to me. His tiny tongue flicks out, licking the tears from my cheeks.

I push him away, not wanting any comfort. Not now.

But he's persistent, his little paws scrabbling at my lap as he continues his gentle ministrations. Eventually, I relent. My arms wrap around his small frame and I pull him close, relishing the warmth of his body against mine.

His kisses are relentless and earnest, each one a small balm for my wounded soul. I bury my face in his fur, letting the steady rhythm of his breathing anchor me.

In that moment of raw vulnerability, a realization dawns on me. I'm not truly alone. My heart may be shattered into a million pieces, but I am still here—whole and capable of healing. And the circus wasn't just Logan's dream.

It became mine too. Every performer put their heart and soul into this show we've been preparing for. They deserve to see it come to life, regardless of what happens next.

I lift my head and wipe away the remaining tears with the back of my hand. Tricks looks up at me with those big, trusting eyes, and determination sparks inside me.

I stand up slowly, still clutching Tricks close to my chest. My steps are hesitant at first but grow steadier with each stride. There's work to be done and people counting on me.

Logan may have left a void in my heart but that doesn't mean I have to abandon everything we built together. The performers worked so freaking hard on the new show. For that matter, so did I. We deserve to have the debut, no matter what happens after.

 After all, it's the first rule of the circus…

 The show must go on.

CHAPTER SEVENTEEN

I STAND AT the entrance of the big tent, my hands trembling slightly as I grip the thick canvas flap. The familiar scent of sawdust and excitement fills my nostrils. Tonight it's tinged with something bittersweet.

Backstage, Cirque des Miroirs buzzes with pre-show energy. Performers dash back and forth, adjusting costumes and applying last-minute makeup. The air crackles with anticipation, a palpable electricity that would make my heart race.

Unfortunately, my heart's already pounding for a different reason.

From the corner, I scan the crowd, searching for a face I know I won't find. Logan's absence hurts like a physical ache, a hollow space where he should be standing, proud and tall, overseeing our triumph. At least I hope it'll be a triumph.

A fresh wave of pain courses through me.

The only reason I did this was for him. Now I'm alone.

And the reputation of the entire circus hangs on my desperate fever dream.

I shake my head, forcing the thoughts away. This isn't about me or Logan. It's about every person who's poured their heart and soul into this show. They deserve my full attention, my unwavering support.

Taking a deep breath, I step into the organized chaos backstage. Caterina rushes past, her Juliet costume a swirl of delicate fabric and sparkling gems.

"The rigging!" she calls out, her eyes wide with a mix of excitement and nerves.

I hold up a hand. "I'll check on it."

She nods and dashes off. I make my way to the tech area, my mind shifting into problem-solving mode. There's no room for personal emotions now. The show demands my full attention, and I'm determined to give it nothing less.

As I work through last-minute adjustments, pride builds inside me. Despite everything— Logan's absence, the town's hostility, my own broken heart—we've created something truly magical here.

The music swells, signaling the start of the show.

I take my place in the wings, ready to guide our Romeo and Juliet through their star-crossed journey. For the next few hours, at least, I can lose myself in the story we've woven together.

I hold my breath as the lights dim and the audience falls silent.

The curtain rises, revealing Travis in his clown costume, his face painted with an exaggerated grin that belies any nervousness. This is his moment, our moment, to prove that Cirque des Miroirs is more than just Logan's vision.

Travis ambles across the stage, his oversized shoes flopping comically with each step. I can't help but smile, remembering the shy boy I once defended in Forrester. Now he's commanding the spotlight, drawing laughter from the crowd as he "accidentally" bumps into another clown holding a bucket. It tips over, Travis in a shower of glitter-infused water. The audience gasps, then erupts in delighted giggles as Travis sputters and shakes like a wet dog.

The other clown's face contorts in mock anger, and he grabs a mop, chasing Travis around the ring. Their slapstick chase transforms seamlessly into our reimagined "fight scene." Acrobats in jewel-toned Montague and Capulet costumes emerge from hidden trapdoors, joining the fray. My heart swells with pride as they execute the complex routine we've spent weeks perfecting.

The giant swings creak into motion, and I hold my breath.

The first acrobat soars through the air, twisting and turning in a series of complex moves before tumbling gracefully to the ground. Yes! Exhilaration rushes through me.

The audience gasps and cheers with each death-defying leap.

I scan their faces, seeing wonder and awe replace the suspicion and hostility that's haunted us since arriving in Forrester. In this instant, there's only the magic of the circus, the thrill of watching these incredible performers push the boundaries of what's possible.

As the scene reaches its crescendo, with acrobats flying in intricate patterns above the ring, I realize I'm grinning so hard my cheeks hurt. We did it. We've created something beautiful, something that transcends all the ugliness we've faced.

My heart swells with joy as I see the audience's reactions, their faces filled with wonder and amazement. The sea of eyes wide with awe, mouths slightly agape, mirrors the very magic we've poured into this performance. Each gasp, each cheer, fuels the fire inside me, pushing aside the shadows of doubt and despair that have haunted me for weeks.

There are juggling acts, acrobatics, and a giant wheel controlled by a man around the stage. In between, Romeo and Juliet step out for emotional vignettes that move the story.

A gymnast finishes his act, beaming at the crowd, his smile reflecting their joy.

Cat stands ready for her entrance as Juliet, her dark eyes sparkling. She catches my gaze and gives a subtle nod. We share an unspoken understanding—tonight is about more than just the performance. It's about proving to ourselves and everyone else that we are strong, resilient, capable of beauty even in the face of adversity.

As the first act draws to a close, I slip out from behind the curtains and make my way toward the audience area. I want to feel their energy up close, to soak in their reactions as we transition into the heart of our story.

"Did you see that?"

"My toxic trait is thinking I could do that."

"You'd break your neck."

I grin, unable to resist the raw enthusiasm of the crowd. There were grueling rehearsals, the sleepless nights, constant pressure. They all led to this moment.

Cat steps onto the stage. She embodies Juliet with every fiber of her being—graceful yet fierce, vulnerable yet unyielding.

Felix enters as Romeo, his usual swagger replaced by a tender intensity that makes my breath catch. Together they weave a tale of love and loss that resonates deeply with me—our own struggles reflected in Shakespeare's timeless story.

The audience leans forward collectively as Caterina and Felix share their first kiss—a delicate brush of lips that holds all the promise and heartbreak of young love. The air is thick with emotion; it pulses around us like a living thing.

My breath catches as the grand finale approaches. Tricks sits obediently at my feet, his little tail wagging. He knows it's coming.

I kneel down, adjusting his miniature friar's robe one last time.

"You ready, buddy?" I whisper, scratching behind his ear. His tongue lolls out in response, and I can't help but smile. "Show them what you've got."

As the cue comes, I give Tricks a gentle nudge. He trots out onto the stage, his tiny paws barely making a sound on the sawdust-covered floor. The audience's reaction is immediate—a wave of laughter and delighted gasps ripples through the tent.

Tricks prances around Felix and Cat, who accept his poison with total seriousness, playing their roles to perfection. His antics provide a stark contrast to the tragic scene, his tail wagging furiously as he performs the tricks we've practiced countless times.

He sits up on his hind legs, "praying" over the bodies with his front paws clasped together. Then he rolls over, playing dead himself for a moment before springing back up and yipping cheerfully. The crowd eats it up, their laughter a balm to my frayed nerves.

As Tricks makes a victory lap around the center ring, pride surges through me. This little stray I found on the roadside is stealing the show.

The juxtaposition of Tricks's playful energy against the grim tableau creates exactly a compelling vision. It's a reminder of life's unpredictability, how joy and sorrow often dance side by side. About how we have to find laughter in even the darkest times.

The audience erupts in applause.

As I stand at the edge of the performers' entrance, my eyes scan the sea of faces in the audience. The smiles, the wide eyes filled with wonder—they're why we do this. But amidst the crowd, a flicker of movement catches my eye.

I squint, my breath catching in my throat. Could it be…?

Logan.

My heart skips a beat. He said he wasn't coming, that he didn't want to be part of the circus anymore. His words had cut deep, leaving me raw and aching. Yet there he stands, his silhouette unmistakable even in the dim light filtering through the tent.

For a moment, I can't breathe. Hope flares within me, bright and blinding, but it's tempered by the sting of his rejection. The things he said— they still echo in my mind, each one a tiny dagger lodged in my heart.

He moves closer to the entrance, his gaze locked on me. There's something in his eyes—a mix of regret and longing—that makes my chest tighten. I want to run to him, to demand answers and assurances.

Instead, I stay rooted to the spot, torn between hope and hurt.

The final act crescendos around us, performers spinning and leaping with an intensity that matches my swirling emotions. I glance back at them, at Caterina and Felix as they execute their roles with flawless precision. This is what we've built together—Logan and me—and it's beautiful beyond words.

Yet here he is now, on the periphery of our world.

Does he regret leaving? Is he here to reclaim his place in the circus?

I swallow hard, pushing down the whirlwind inside me. Whatever happens next—whether Logan steps back into my life or remains apart—I have to focus on this moment, on finishing this performance with all the strength and passion we've mustered.

CHAPTER EIGHTEEN

T HE FINAL ACT concludes with a resounding applause that reverberates through the tent, echoing the pounding of my heart. I step into the ring, the bright lights illuminating every corner, every face turned toward us in admiration. The performers gather around me, their eyes shining with a mixture of relief and triumph.

Cat is the first to reach me, her face flushed with exhilaration. "You did it!" she exclaims, throwing her arms around me in a tight hug.

Her enthusiasm is infectious, and I can't help but laugh as I hug her back.

"We all did," I say. "You were an incredible Juliet."

Felix swaggers over, exhilaration making him look almost happy. Almost, because he's always got that tragic air. Which is what made him so great at his role. "What about Romeo?"

"Couldn't have done it without you and your terrible life decisions."

Wolfgang steps forward, his usual stoic demeanor softened by pride. "Sienna, you did a good thing here. You kept us together when everything was falling apart."

I swallow the lump in my throat. "You're a family."

Cat's eyes glisten. "*We* are a family."

"Three cheers for our creative director," Felix says.

No one misses a beat. Performers are busy changing, some heading out to sign autographs for the kids. There are operations folks back here. Everyone stops to shout, "Hip hip hooray," and then shout and hoot in my general direction.

Goose bumps run over my skin. Shit.

"Who brought onions in here?" I say, wiping my eyes. "It's probably bad luck to have them backstage in a circus, like entering the ring on your right foot."

"Left foot," someone calls.

This sets off a round of arguing over the many superstitions that make up the circus. No one seems to doubt their validity. The arguments seem to be more along the lines of which ones lead to worse luck than the others.

Tricks barks happily at our feet, wagging his tail to join in the discussion.

I give a watery laugh.

Cat ruffles his fur and showers him with praise for bringing her poison. The circus might have been Logan's dream initially, but tonight proved it's ours too—every single one of us.

Logan steps into view. My heart pounds. The chatter among the cast dies instantly, all eyes turning to him. He looks stark and severe, but he's here. That's all that matters.

"You came," I whisper, barely able to get the words out.

He nods, his gaze sweeping over the assembled performers. "I couldn't miss this," he says, his voice rough with emotion. "The show was incredible. Each one of you performed a miracle tonight."

Caterina is the first to break the spell. She rushes forward, wrapping her arms around Logan in a fierce hug. "Boss!" she exclaims, her voice muffled against his chest.

That seems to open the floodgates. The rest of the cast surges forward, surrounding Logan with hugs, handshakes, and words of welcome. I hang back, watching as he's enveloped by the love and admiration of our circus family.

Felix claps Logan on the shoulder, grinning. "Knew you couldn't stay away for long."

Logan's lips quirk in a small smile, but I can see the strain behind it. He's been through hell, and it shows in every line of his face, every careful movement.

His eyes find mine over the heads of the others, and for a moment, no one else exists.

"You were amazing tonight," he says.

I try to act like this is a very normal thing, me meeting him after just planning an entire freaking show at which some tickets went for five thousand dollars. In the circus that he owns. I shove my hand in my hair so he can't see it tremble. "Glad it looked cool, because I was making that shit up as I went along."

His smile dims. "You always try to put down your achievements. You still get credit for it if you only did it to survive, only fought back because the world started it. You are incredible. And talented. And also, I have to admit, very forgiving."

I raise an eyebrow. "Am I?"

"Extremely."

"I don't know if that's a particular trait of mine."

"You forgive me for acting like an ass, for example."

"That seems like a lot to forgive."

"Especially without a proper apology." He reaches out, his fingers brushing against mine. It's such a small gesture, but it sends shivers down my spine. "I'm so fucking sorry. I thought I needed space or time or whatever the fuck would make me the person you fell in love with."

My heart wrenches. Maybe I wanted an apology. Needed one. It still breaks my heart. "Logan."

"I didn't understand that you didn't need that person. He wasn't real, anymore, the one so damned sure of himself he could kiss a beautiful girl and offer her a ride out of town and not think it would change anything. That he wouldn't have to face his demons."

"Your demons are pretty evil."

"What I didn't know is that you never fell for that guy. He was a myth, but you always saw the real me. With all my shadows and bullshit. With everything. That's how you wanted me. I was just me."

I look up at him, my heart in my throat.

"It's our dream now," he says. "Yours. Mine. If you'll have me."

The words hang between us, heavy with promise and unspoken fears.

"I'm afraid you're not real," I confess, my voice barely more than a whisper.

His hand tightens around mine. "We'll talk more," he replies, his gaze never leaving mine. "I have some things I need to say."

Logan greets each and every cast member by name. His voice carries a quiet authority, but there's warmth in it too, a genuine gratitude that makes everyone he speaks to stand a little taller.

"Your juggling was on point tonight."

"Great job. Your tumbling act was gorgeous."

One by one, they beam at him, soaking up his praise. I can't blame them—Logan's approval means everything to this ragtag family of ours. But impatience gnaws at me. I need to talk to him, need to understand what he's thinking after everything we've been through.

Finally, the tent starts to empty out. Performers trickle away in pairs and small groups, their laughter and chatter fading into the night. The stands are deserted now, wooden benches standing silent sentinel under the moonlight that filters through the tent flap.

Logan wraps his arms around me, pulling me close. His embrace is warm, solid, grounding. The scent of him—sawdust and sweat—fills my senses, a heady reminder of everything we've fought for.

"Thank you for the beautiful show," he murmurs against my hair. His voice is thick with emotion, every word a caress. "I can't tell you how much it means to me. How much you mean to me."

My heart pounds in my chest, each beat echoing his words. I tilt my head back to look up at him, my eyes searching his face for any hint of the pain that still lingers beneath the surface.

"I learned how to believe in the circus from you," I confess, my voice trembling with sincerity and love. "You've always been the heart of this place, Logan. You taught me what it means to have faith in something bigger than ourselves."

His gaze intensifies, dark eyes locking on to mine with an intensity that sends shivers down my spine. The air between us crackles with anticipation, every breath we take drawing us closer together.

"You kept it alive," he whispers, his voice rough and desperate. "You kept *me* alive."

The distance between us disappears as we slowly lean in, our breaths mingling in the scant space left between our lips. Time seems to stretch and contract all at once, each second an eternity as we hover on the brink.

Then our lips meet in a passionate and desperate kiss. It's not just a kiss; it's a promise, a release, a thousand unsaid words and shared pains. His lips are soft but insistent against mine, and I respond with equal fervor, pouring everything into that connection.

His hands tangle in my hair, pulling me even closer if that's possible. My fingers curl into the fabric of his shirt, holding on to him like he's my lifeline.

My hands instinctively find their way to Logan's chest, loving the warmth of his skin beneath my fingertips. His heart beats steadily against my palm, a rhythm that matches my own racing pulse. Our bodies press against each other, the heat between us growing with every passing second.

Logan's hands roam over my body, his touch igniting a fire within me. He traces the curve of my waist, the dip of my hips, and the swell of my breasts. Each caress sends a shiver down my spine, leaving me breathless and wanting more.

I gasp as his fingers brush against the sensitive skin of my neck, sending a jolt of electricity through my body. He leans in closer, his lips finding mine in a passionate kiss that leaves me dizzy with desire. Our tongues dance together, exploring and tasting each other with a sense of urgency that only heightens the intensity of our connection.

The sounds of our heavy breathing and whispered words of sex fill the empty tent, creating an intimate symphony that echoes through the air. I can feel the rough fabric of Logan's shirt beneath my hands, the texture contrasting with the smoothness of his skin. I tug at the hem, pulling it up and over his head, revealing the toned muscles of his chest and stomach.

Logan's hands move to the zipper of my dress, slowly sliding it down and exposing the lace of my bra. He cups my breasts in his hands, his thumbs brushing against my nipples through the thin fabric. I moan softly, arching my back and pressing myself further into his touch.

His lips leave mine, trailing kisses down my neck and across my collarbone. I tilt my head back, giving him better access as he continues his exploration. His mouth finds the sensitive spot just below my ear, and I gasp as he nips and suckles at the skin there.

My hands roam over his body, over the strength and power that lies beneath the surface. I trace the lines of his tattoos, following the intricate patterns and designs that cover his arms and shoulders. Each one tells a story, a piece of the puzzle that is Logan Whitmere.

As our bodies move together, tension builds in the air. The fire that Logan ignited within me is now a raging inferno, consuming every thought and desire. I want him more than I've ever wanted anything in my life, and he has the same urgency.

Logan's hands move to the waistband of my panties, sliding them down my legs and leaving me completely exposed. I step out of them, kicking them aside as I wrap my arms around his neck. He lifts me up, carrying me over to a nearby crate and setting me down on top of it.

Rough wood abrades my skin, the texture adding to the sensory overload that is consuming me. Logan's hands are everywhere, touching and caressing every inch of my body. His cock presses against me. I need him inside me.

"Logan," I whisper, my voice barely audible above the sound of our heavy breathing. "I need you."

He looks into my eyes, his gaze filled with desire and love. "I need you too, Sienna," he replies, his voice husky with emotion.

And with that, he enters me, filling me completely and sending waves of pleasure coursing through my body. I wrap my legs around his waist, pulling him closer as we move together in perfect harmony. The sounds of our lovemaking fill the tent, a symphony of passion and desire that echoes through the air.

My body arches in pleasure as Logan's lips trail down my neck, leaving a trail of fiery kisses in their wake. The roughness of his stubble against my soft skin makes me burn. Each touch ignites a new fire within me. The center stage, bathed in moonlight, becomes our sanctuary, the sawdust and the faint scent of popcorn our bizarrely beautiful aphrodisiac.

Logan's hands roam over my body, tracing every curve and line as if it were a sacred ground. His touch is rough yet gentle, a contradiction that drives me wild.

Logan's mouth moves from mine, trailing kisses down my neck, his stubble scraping lightly against my skin. I shiver, my breath hitching as he lingers on the sensitive spot where my neck meets my shoulder. His hands roam over my body, strong and sure, tracing the curve of my waist, the swell of my hips.

He lifts me effortlessly, setting me down on the edge of a prop table, the wood rough and cool against my bare thighs. His eyes, dark and intense, lock on to mine as he kneels before me. My heart pounds in my chest, anticipation coursing through my veins like wildfire.

Logan's hands slide up my thighs, his touch firm yet gentle. He runs his hands up my bare legs, possessing me inch by inch. I can feel the heat of his breath against my skin, sending shivers of pleasure up my spine.

His gaze never leaves mine as he leans in, his breath hot against my most intimate place. I gasp as his tongue flicks out, tasting me, teasing me. He starts slow, his tongue tracing the length of me, exploring every fold and crevice. My hands grip the edge of the table, knuckles white, as waves of pleasure wash over me.

Logan's pace quickens, his tongue delving deeper, his lips sucking and nipping at my sensitive flesh. I can feel the tension building within me, a coil winding tighter and tighter, threatening to snap at any moment. My breath comes in ragged gasps, my moans echoing through the empty tent.

His hands grip my thighs, spreading me wider, giving him better access. He groans against me, the vibration sending shockwaves of pleasure through my body. I can feel his hunger, his desire, matching my own. His tongue circles my clit, applying just the right amount of pressure, driving me closer and closer to the edge.

My body arches, my hips bucking against his mouth as the coil snaps. Waves of intense pleasure crash over me, leaving me breathless and shaking. Logan's grip on my thighs tightens, holding me in place as he continues to lick and suck, drawing out every last drop of my orgasm.

I collapse back onto the table, my body limp and sated. Logan stands, his eyes never leaving mine as he wipes his mouth with the back of his hand. The hunger in his gaze sends a fresh wave of desire coursing through me, and I know that this night is far from over.

Our bodies entwine in a passionate embrace, our movements synchronized and filled with raw intensity. The world around us fades away, leaving only the two of us, our breaths mingling, our hearts beating as one. Logan's lips find mine, his kiss hungry and demanding, stealing the very air from my lungs.

I can feel the strength in his body as he moves against me, his muscles taut and defined. Our bodies move in perfect harmony, our love and desire intertwining like the acrobats in the air. Each thrust, each touch, each kiss is a dance, a performance that only we understand.

The climax of our lovemaking is met with a shared release, our bodies trembling with the intensity of our connection. Logan's grip on me tightens, his fingers digging into my flesh as he holds on to me like I'm his lifeline. I cling to him just as fiercely, my nails raking down his back, marking him as mine.

Our breaths come in ragged gasps, our hearts pounding in our chests. The world around us is silent, the only sound the echo of our shared pleasure. Logan's forehead rests against mine, his eyes locked on to mine, the depth of emotion in them stealing my breath away.

"Sienna," he whispers, his voice hoarse with desire and something more, something deeper. I can see it in his eyes, feel it in his touch. This isn't just sex; it's a promise, a vow. It's love in its rawest, most primal form.

Our breaths slowly return to normal as we lie entwined on the center stage, the faint scent of sawdust and greasepaint mingling with the aftermath of our passion. Logan's arm is draped over me, his fingers lightly tracing patterns on my bare skin. The echoes of our lovemaking still hum through my body, a sweet reminder of our connection.

I tilt my head to look at him, finding his eyes

already on me. There's a softness in his gaze that I haven't seen in a long time, a vulnerability that makes my heart ache.

"You were amazing tonight," he murmurs, his voice filled with genuine admiration.

I smile, brushing a strand of hair away from his forehead. "I couldn't have done it without you."

Logan shakes his head gently. "No, Sienna. This was all you. You kept the circus alive when I couldn't. You gave everyone hope."

His words fill me with warmth, a sense of pride swelling in my chest. "I did it for us," I whisper. "For this family we've built together."

He leans in, pressing a tender kiss to my lips. It's soft and slow, a stark contrast to the intensity we shared moments ago. "I love you," he says against my mouth, the words wrapping around my heart like a warm embrace.

"I love you too," I reply, my voice steady and sure. "More than anything."

Logan's fingers brush against my cheek, his touch featherlight. "Thank you," he whispers, his eyes searching mine for understanding. "For not giving up on me. On us."

I shake my head slightly, tears pricking at the corners of my eyes. "I could never give up on you,

Logan. You're everything to me."

His lips curl into a small smile, one that reaches his eyes and fills them with a spark of hope. "And you're everything to me," he says.

We lie there in silence for a while longer, simply basking in each other's presence. The world outside the tent seems far away and insignificant compared to the love and gratitude that fills this space between us.

As our breaths even out and our bodies relax further into each other's embrace, I feel a newfound sense of strength and hope blooming within me. We've faced so much together and come out stronger on the other side.

"Together," Logan whispers into the quiet night.

"Always," I respond, tightening my hold on him as if to anchor myself to this moment forever.

CHAPTER NINETEEN

SIT AT the kitchen table, a cup of tea in front of me.

How much do I look like my mother? Her skin is more wrinkled. Her hair is shorter and curled tight, though still fully black, because she dyed it once gray hairs started coming in. We are from different generations, different lives, but similar. Too similar.

Sitting here with tea always felt like giving in, like submitting to fate.

What I didn't understand is that fate does not give a fuck about teacups. It's going to grab hold of me and shake. Which it did. So now I'm taking the solace where I can find it, which helps me understand her. Perhaps there was a part of her that felt defeated, but there was another part that knew that even a few minutes of peace was worth having.

Though she doesn't seem peaceful now.

She fidgets with her hands, fingers twisting and turning as if trying to unravel the knots of our shared past. The silence between us is thick, heavy with lingering shadows.

She takes a deep breath. "I need to tell you something."

I nod, the anticipation knotting in my stomach. I mean, the last time she confessed something it was murder. Even if it was justified, it's still enough to make me nervous. "Okay, but if it's a felony, I hope you spiked the tea, because I'm going to need it."

"I'm not sorry that I unplugged Patrick from life support," she says, the words hanging in the air like a final judgment. "He needed to be stopped, but I think I might have done it anyway. Even if he would never hit me again. Because he deserved it."

A sob catches in my throat, but it's not from sadness.

It's relief, pure and unfiltered. Justice could be a strange beast. It grabbed hold of Logan's leg by the teeth while letting my father go free for decades. Then again, I suppose justice wasn't really some abstract concept. It was just people, in the end. People like Sheriff Dunham and Logan, one obsessed with power, the other with kindness.

And my mother, who found her own closure.

"Mom. Did you think I would judge you for that?"

Banyu's eyes well up with tears as she continues, her voice cracking under the weight of her confession. "I judge myself. It's a sin. For years, I endured his abuse. The beatings, the insults… the constant fear that consumed me every single day."

Her hands shake as she speaks, and I reach out to hold them, grounding her in this moment. "I wish you had talked to me about it before."

"You were a child," she says, her voice barely above a whisper. "I tried to protect you. I know I wasn't always able to do that."

I squeeze her hands tighter, offering silent support as my own tears mix with hers. There were times I would never tell her about. Times she would never tell me about. Bruises, both visible and hidden, that we never talked about. A thousand secrets in this house.

Nothing, not even unplugging life support, will unleash them.

Except that the heavy shades have been pulled back.

The windows are cracked open, autumn giving us a cool day as a little treat.

"He told me he would kill you. I was so relieved when you left. Angry. Sad. I missed you, but it also meant you were safe. Finally, safe."

Tears fill my eyes. "Don't."

"I didn't care if they put me in jail."

I shudder at the thought of my mom in Sheriff Dunham's oily clutches. "Well, I care."

She reaches out, her hand trembling. Her fingers are cold, but they squeeze mine tightly, anchoring us both in this fragile moment. "When I did it, I realized my mistake. That I should have done it years ago. I could have put poison in his coffee. Or used a steak knife on his heart. Or I could have learned to drive and hit him with the truck."

"Wow, empowerment is really bloodthirsty."

Tears stream down her cheeks. "I'm sorry for not killing him sooner."

A sob hitches my breath, but I force it down. Someone's gotta keep this from turning maudlin. "I appreciate that, but I'm glad you aren't in jail. And I'm not only talking about the bars in the county jail cell. I'm talking about the one you put yourself in."

She nods slowly. "Yes. Me, too."

"I love you," I say, for probably the first time.

We aren't exactly a cuddly household. She's never said it to me, either, though I never knew whether that was because of my father's abuse or whether it was an ingrained cultural stoicism.

Her grip tightens on my hand. "And I you, Sienna."

So probably the stoicism thing.

I lean over and rest my head on her shoulder, enjoying the warmth of her body against mine. For a moment, everything else fades away—the circus, even the weight of our past. It's just us, mother and daughter, finding solace in each other's presence.

This is a turning point for both of us.

Mom's eyes well up with tears, shimmering in the dim light of our kitchen. I can see the depth of her emotions swirling there—relief, gratitude, love. It's a sight that breaks my heart and heals it all at once.

Banyu reaches out and cups my face with her trembling hand. "You've always been so strong," she whispers. "Even when I couldn't be."

The warmth of her touch melts the last of my defenses. I lean into her hand, closing my eyes for a brief moment of peace. "I learned from you," I murmur.

"Sienna," she says, her voice thick with emotion. "Will you still leave?"

I tighten my grip on her hand, grounding us both in this fragile moment. "Yes, but I'll come back and visit you. I promise."

As we stand up from the table, she pulls me into a tight embrace. The scent of her familiar perfume wraps around me like a comforting blanket.

For the first time in forever, I feel truly safe in her arms.

"So," I say, "what if we cracked open that china cabinet?"

She gives me a severe expression. "Sienna."

"What? I mean, I want to set them free symbolically from their glass prison."

"You just want to play with them," she accuses, but there's no heat.

"We can do both at the same time."

Despite the levity of the moment, it's still a surprise when she actually walks to the cabinet filled with delicate porcelain dolls that have watched over us for years.

The dancer who wears a colorful sari in purple and silk from India.

The Mexican doll in a charro outfit with braids in red ribbons.

The little Dutch girl with her basket of tulips

and pointed hat.

She takes each doll out, sharing the stories she wove about each one as she hand-sewed their outfits, using books from the library as her guide. I never saw her make one. She never did, after the cabinet was full. And after my father destroyed her hope.

It's a part of her life that she's never shared with me. It moves me beyond words to gently touch each face, to stroke their hair, to hold them. I'm finally safe with her—and the reverse is true, as well. That's what it means for her to share these dolls. That she feels safe with me, too. When we're done, we place each doll carefully in its place.

Their stories have already been told.

The story they watch through the glass, the one my mother weaves with her own life, is still unfolding. It looks beautiful and bright.

CHAPTER TWENTY

I STAND ON the hillside, my hand intertwined with Logan's as we watch the circus pack up. The colorful tents fold like origami, disappearing into trucks. Workers scurry about, their laughter and chatter carried on the breeze, but my attention is on the phone in my hand. The screen glows with an article that makes my heart race.

"You need to see this," I say.

He looks down as I start reading aloud.

"*Court Clowns Around: Circus Owner Cleared of All Charges,*" I read. "*In a stunning turn of events, Logan Whitmere, owner of Cirque des Miroirs, has been exonerated of all charges related to the assault and subsequent death of Patrick Cole.*"

Logan's grip on my hand tightens. "Damn. Guess it's real."

"*Justice takes center ring,*" I continue, "*as evi-*

dence presented revealed the corruption of local officials which is now currently under investigation. The forensic lab confirmed that evidence had been manufactured, including the crowbar allegedly used in the assault."

His eyebrows rise. "Coming in a little late with that, forensics lab."

"Okay, someone at the *Forrester Independent* was having way too much fun with these puns. *Both Sheriff Dunham and the county attorney's office walk a tightrope. Though it remains to be seen who will take the lion's share of the blame.*"

He wraps an arm around my shoulders, pulling me close.

"*In lighter news, the community has rallied behind the circus, which debuted a new show to critical acclaim only days after Whitmere was released from custody. Which just proves that the "Big Top" tent can hold up even with the highest stakes.*" I groan. "I've never understood puns. Like, we don't even have lions."

I lower the phone and look up at Logan.

His eyes are shining with unshed tears.

My throat clenches. "Wait. I didn't mean to make you sad."

"You didn't," he says, his voice thick.

Love swells inside me. Along with pride.

Even if they did have to say it like a cheesy freaking T-shirt.

He holds me close, turning to watch our circus family pack up. Profound relief washes over me. The weight we've carried for so long is finally lifted.

Logan kisses my forehead gently. "Here's to new beginnings."

I smile up at him. "Here's to us."

Maisie shows up just as the last of the tents come down, her blue eyes gleaming with excitement. She practically bounces over to us, a ball of energy wrapped in blonde curls. "Have you seen the news?" she asks.

"We were just reading it," I tell her.

"And there's more. I'm going to be your official PR representative."

"I'm sorry," I say. "Don't you mean that you're going to juggle the press?"

She looks confused. "What?"

"Don't ask." Logan looks amused and resigned. "And if you want the job, you're hired. We'll probably need it now that you've catapulted us to internet stardom."

She grins. "Your performers get all the credit. We can do behind-the-scenes videos, interactive social media posts, live streams of rehearsals. This is going to rock."

I study my friend's expression. "You're really serious about this? I mean, I understand why I wanted to leave town, but you love it here."

"Absolutely. It gives me an excuse to stick around a certain grumpy asshole."

I glance over at Wolfgang, who stands a little ways off, his knife glinting in the late afternoon sun as he expertly flips it through his fingers. "Get it, girl."

She takes a deep breath, her eyes scanning the circus grounds. "Plus, you know. I'm ready to see a little bit more of the world. Turns out Forrester's kind of shitty, what with the whole fake-evidence, corrupt-sheriff thing."

Logan snorts.

"We are going to come back, though," I warn her. "I have not been able to convince my mom about the miracles of modern plumbing in RVs, so I have to visit."

Maisie beams at me. "Perfect. I'll want to visit my parents, anyway."

Her blonde curls bounce as she walks beside Wolfgang, her chatter filling the air like birdsong. Next to her, Wolfgang's tall, imposing figure moves with a quiet, probably lethal grace, his serious demeanor a stark contrast to her effervescence.

Logan watches them, his expression pensive. "She'll make a good addition."

"To the circus or to Wolfgang?"

"To both."

I grin. "It's funny how love works, isn't it?"

"Funny," he agrees, but he's not looking at them.

He's looking at me.

Warmth spreads through me. His arm wraps around my waist, and I lean into him, feeling his steady heartbeat against my side. For the first time in forever, the future looks bright. "So, we're going to choose the tour stops soon. Everyone wants the show."

"We'll tour until you're ready to stop."

Surprise lifts my eyebrows. "Why would I want to stop?"

"Eventually you might prefer life off the road."

"Where would we go then?"

"The farm," he replies without hesitation.

My lips curve. "The farm?"

"It's a real place."

I rest my head on his shoulder, savoring the picture he's painted. A sense of contentment washes over me. "I'd like that. Assuming it's not a code name for some kind of LSD trip."

Logan turns to face me, his eyes intense and amused. "It's a real place. A beautiful place, but it's not my home. That's wherever you are."

His hands frame my face, his touch gentle yet firm, as if he's afraid I might slip away. His thumb brushes against my cheek, tracing a path down to my lips. I close my eyes, leaning into his caress, enjoying the rough calluses on his fingers—a testament to a life of hard work, of a circus built rope by rope.

His breath is warm on my skin as he leans in, his lips finding mine in a soft, exploratory kiss. It deepens, becoming more urgent, more passionate. I grant him access, and his tongue sweeps in, dancing with mine in a rhythm that's uniquely ours.

I press closer, my body molding against his.

His heartbeat pounds steady and strong, a comforting drumbeat that reminds me we're alive, we're together. We're home. His hands slide down my back, pulling me tighter, as if he can't get enough.

His lips trail down my neck, leaving a path of fire in their wake.

I gasp, my head falling back, giving him better access.

He takes advantage, his mouth finding that sensitive spot where my neck meets my shoulder. He knows my body so well, knows how to make me shiver with desire.

My hands roam the hard planes beneath his shirt. I tug at the fabric, needing his skin against mine. He pulls the shirt over his head and tosses it aside. My fingers trace the colorful circus tattoos across his biceps and shoulders, each one a story, a piece of him.

"Sunset," he whispers, his voice husky with emotion. It's a promise, a vow. A testament to our shared history, our shared pain, our shared triumphs.

I reach up, pulling him back to me, our lips meeting in a fierce, claiming kiss. In this moment, we're not just two people on a hillside; we're two souls intertwined, healing each other, making each other whole.

I stand there with Logan, the horizon stretching out before us, and my heart swells with a mixture of relief, gratitude, and hope. "You know," I begin, my voice soft but steady, "when I look back at everything we've been through—the violence, the murder charge, the circus. It makes me wonder how we juggled it all."

Logan curses under his breath.

"I'm starting to see the appeal of puns, honestly. We don't need to take everything so seriously. Sometimes you just need to clown around."

"I'm going back to jail."

"Sometimes you're the ringmaster. Sometimes you're the clown." My smile fades. "I'm sorry about Emerson. I never thought that I would—"

"You did nothing wrong."

"He left because of me."

"He left because he's a prick who doesn't like answering to anyone."

"I took over when I had no right to."

"Yes, Sunset. You took over something that was falling apart and made it whole again. You believed in me when I was ready to give up. You showed me what love really means—standing up for what's right against any odds."

"So, you aren't mad at me?"

"Darling, haven't you noticed by now? I'm obsessed with you."

"Mmm, those things don't seem mutually exclusive."

Logan's thumb brushes a tear away from my cheek. "I'm not angry. You stood up against bullies the day we met, remember? It's the first thing I noticed about you."

I swipe the tears from my eyes, trying to play it off. "I thought you noticed my tits."

"That was the second thing."

He proceeds to show me how much he appreciates every square inch of me. And I let him, because he taught me something, too. I already knew how to fight. My God, I'd done enough of it already. And I'm sure there's more in my future, the world being what it is.

The fighting may be necessary, but it's the loving that makes it worth it.

CHAPTER TWENTY-ONE

MELANCHOLIC NOTES FLOAT through the sweet-scented air.

The music room in North Security headquarters is probably worth a few million dollars, judging from the pedigree of some of these instruments. A grand piano dominates the space, its polished surface reflecting the soft light filtering through the filigree curtains. The saxophone was once played by Charlie Parker.

Then there's the Stradivarius that Samantha plays now, her fingers dancing over the strings with masterful ease, coaxing out a haunting melody that seems to wrap itself around my heart and squeeze.

I lean back in the armchair, closing my eyes to better absorb the music. Each note resonates deep within me, stirring emotions I thought I'd buried.

The room is filled with a sense of timelessness, as if there's no beginning or end to the song. The melody weaves through my mind, pulling me back to memories of nights under the circus tent, the thrill of Logan's touch, and the raw hope that drives me forward.

I open my eyes and watch Samantha play, her concentration evident in the way she bites her lower lip. She's led such a different life from me, one of opulence instead of small-town poverty, one of isolation instead of gossip. Her father ignored her rather than beat her. That doesn't make me think she had it easier. Fathers have plenty of ways to fuck up their little girls. The love of a good man isn't required to overcome that, but it sure does help.

Her music speaks to my soul, pooling around the highs and lows of my life.

A sense of clarity settles over me. The notes are like a map guiding me through my tangled thoughts, reminding me why I started this journey in the first place—for love, for freedom, for a chance to build something beautiful out of chaos.

I glance around the room at the framed photographs on the walls—images of Samantha performing in grand concert halls, her face lit with passion and determination. The final notes linger in the air as Samantha's hands still on the keys. She turns to look at me, her expression softening from intense concentration to gentle curiosity.

"You were miles away," she says.

"Just listening."

"Liar," she accuses. "You were thinking of how to incorporate the song into one of your shows, weren't you?"

"So rude of you to be that observant."

She grins. "I was thinking the same thing."

"Right? There's something in it that makes you think of love. Not someone searching. Someone who's already found it and lost it. And they know they'll never have it again."

She shudders. "It's sad."

"You were the one who composed it."

"Yeah, I'm basically Eeyore."

I have to laugh, because it's true. It's also very much not true. She always has a smile on her face and a kind word. It would almost be too Pollyanna, if she didn't also have that deep well of sadness. You can feel it even if you can't see it. And you can definitely hear it in the music she composes.

Samantha begins another piece, lighter and more hopeful this time.

As Samantha's fingers dance over the violin strings, my phone buzzes on the table beside me. I glance down, seeing Logan's name flash across the screen. Uh. Why is he calling me? He was just here like an hour ago. I swipe to open the message.

Come join me in the basement.

That's all it says. No explanation, no details. Just those few words that send a ripple of unease through me. What basement? I stand and walk out as quietly as possible, not wanting to disturb Samantha's practice.

A thought occurs to me. What if he's terse because something is happening with the charges? Is he in trouble again? Shit shit shit.

I descend the stairs, sucking in a breath to see someone who looks scary as hell. He's built like a freaking Mack truck. I knew this place had mercenaries. I've seen them working through the massive obstacle courses across these hills. Then he looks up, and I realize why he's here, in the main residence. His eyes are the same as Liam's. They must be related.

"Hi," I say, hoping they don't go full commando on strangers.

"You must be Sienna," he says.

"Oh shit. Does my reputation precede me?

You don't go to the Forrester Library do you?"

"No reputation. And… also no. What did you do wrong at the library?"

"It's a long story involving a bully and a popcorn machine."

"That only makes me want to know more."

"How did you know my name?"

"I read the HQDRs. The headquarters daily reports."

"Holy shit. Security around here is no joke."

He cracks a small smile. "Absolutely not."

"You must be related to Liam."

"His brother. Elijah."

"Nice to meet you. Now, do you happen to know where the basement is?"

"I'll walk you over, but I expect to hear the popcorn machine story."

I follow him out of the house and around the side, walking through lush green lawns. "Some other time. It takes like a full ten minutes without pauses."

"Then you can tell us at dinner. My wife is coming. Holly got to see the debut of Star-Crossed. She's been dying to meet the person who wrote it."

Oh man, the way his eyes got all dreamy at the mention of his wife. This guy is seriously in love. "Well, I hate to break it to her, but it was kind of a Shakespeare thing."

"She's an author, so I think she values the work of a retelling."

He pauses at a set of metal stairs that descend into the earth.

It looks kind of… scary.

"Is it weird that I've never actually been in a basement before?"

"Nah, they aren't usual in Texas being at sea level and all that. This house was built on a hill, so they could dig into it a little deeper."

"Okay, well, if I die there, I'm coming back to haunt you."

He gives me a salute, only the faintest trace of amusement on his very serious face. Tough crowd. The dim lighting casts long, twisted shadows that seem to reach out from the corners. Each step I take sends a shiver down my spine, the air thick with an unspoken tension. The basement is a different world entirely, removed from the warmth and familiarity of upstairs—a place where secrets lie buried and confrontations come to a head.

My footsteps echo in the cavernous space, bouncing off the cold stone walls and amplifying the sense of isolation. Please be something fun, I think to myself. Like a fondue bar. Or a giant ball pit. Nope, it's exactly as horrifying as you'd expect a basement to be. I spot Logan first—his tall, imposing figure framed by the flickering light of a single bulb.

And then I see Kyle.

He's restrained, his hands bound behind his back with thick rope. His usual smug demeanor is replaced by a mix of fear and defiance. His eyes dart around the room before settling on me, narrowing with urgency.

Logan's jaw clenches as he turns his gaze toward me. "Sunset."

I step closer, my heart pounding in my chest. The tension between them is palpable, a live wire crackling with energy. It's in the way Logan's muscles tense, the way Kyle's eyes flicker with panic.

"Um. Hi. What's going on?"

Kyle scoffs, trying to muster some semblance of bravado despite his predicament. "Your boyfriend here thinks he can scare me," he says, a tremor in his voice that's betraying his words. "He's going to be cut into pieces by the time I'm done with him."

Logan takes a step forward, his eyes locked on to Kyle with an intensity that sends a chill down my spine. "You don't know what real fear is," he says quietly, but every word is laced with menace.

I move closer to Logan, placing a hand on his arm in an attempt to ground him—to remind him that we're in this together. "Hey, big guy," I say softly, trying to break through the red haze of his anger. "Did they not tell you about the local laws? It's a funny custom we have here in Forrester that we try not to torture the neighbors."

Kyle sneers at me from his restrained position. "You're all dead."

I follow his line of sight to see Liam sitting in the corner. He's leaned back, focused but clearly letting his friend take the lead right now.

I turn my attention back to Logan. His eyes meet mine, and for a moment, I see the man I fell in love with—the man who built a home for so many lost souls under that circus tent. "We're outside of Forrester city *and* county limits," he says. "And more importantly, I got him for you. As a present."

"Like a threesome kind of thing? Because in that case, I have my period."

His lips quirk. "Like a threesome if one of them has their dreams destroyed."

Kyle watches us with narrowed eyes. "You

have nothing on me."

He steps back. It's a silent offering, a transfer of power.

The freedom to face my enemy and come out on the other side.

My gaze locks with Kyle's. His sneer falters.

Fear flickers in his eyes, but it's quickly masked by his usual arrogance.

"Do you remember how we first met?" I ask him. "You were sitting all alone because you kept trying to make everyone eat glue. So I went and sat with you. You threatened to make me eat glue, but I told you I'd break your fingers."

Kyle shifts against his restraints but keeps his chin up. "What's your point?"

"We became friends. Best friends, along with Travis. Honestly, I don't know what would have happened if we'd stayed that way. Maybe Travis and I could have actually been accepted. Or maybe the town wasn't ready for an Asian American and a gay guy, even if you'd stood by our side. It would have been nice to find out."

His bravado wavers, and I see a bead of sweat trickle down his temple. He knows he's cornered, but he still tries to maintain his defiance. "We grew apart. It didn't mean anything."

"You didn't grow at all. You just kept making

people eat glue, except instead of glue, it was the assholes' fists." I glance at Logan. "Where are they, by the way?"

"In jail. I only managed to get them to hold off on arresting Kyle for the night."

His eyes widen. "Arrest? For what? Wait until my uncle finds out."

"Your uncle is about to get disbarred," Logan says, sounding bored.

I grin at him. "You know, some guys just get their girls flowers."

"Boring. Trite. And dead in a few days."

"Aww. Instead you got me revenge. That's so sweet."

Kyle's eyes widen. "You guys are fucking insane."

Logan grabs the front of Kyle's shirt, yanking him forward. The metal feet of the chair scrape as his body rocks. The movement catches him off guard, and fear flashes in his eyes. "Your scholarship?" Logan says. "Gone."

Kyle's bravado crumbles, replaced by a look of shock and disbelief. "You're lying," he whispers, but there's no conviction in his voice.

Logan releases him, stepping back.

Kyle's shoulders slump, his cocky façade giving way to vulnerability. "This... this isn't fair," he says, as if anyone cares.

I roll my eyes. "Was it fair when you tormented others?"

Kyle's emotions war across his face—anger, frustration, and finally, a glimmer of despair. He looks up at me, and for the first time, I see him not as the untouchable bully, but as a scared, horrible, small person. One who's finally facing the consequences.

I watch as Kyle grapples with this new reality.

The basement falls silent, save for his ragged breathing.

"Go on," Logan says to me.

I look around the dimly lit space. "Go on and what?"

"Go on and punch him."

"Okay, I just feel like this should have had stage directions. Like you planned a whole thing, and I'm trying to keep up."

Logan grins. "Thumb on the outside of your fingers. Aim for the soft part of the eye. Do not, under any circumstances, break your fingers. It really kills the high."

"Oh, please. I know how to punch a guy."

"Excellent."

I turn to face Kyle, who might be trying to act brave? It's hard to tell when his lower lip is quivering like that. Possibly I should care about that, but he's hurt enough people that I don't. Travis. Then Logan.

Along with, you know, me. If I were to value myself.

Which I found hard to do before. A lot of abuse victims struggle with that, I've learned, but I'm getting better at it with practice.

Having Logan value me sets a good example.

Anticipation pulses through my veins. I have actually punched Kyle before, but it's always been in an imminent-danger, self-defense way. Winding up feels new.

I pause. "Is it cheating if he's tied up?"

"Were you tied up in the trunk of his car?"

"Good point."

Kyle snorts. "You're not going to do it."

Which is just the motivation I needed.

I make a fist, pull back, and pop him right in the eye.

He lets out a yelp that's surprisingly high-pitched.

"Okay, that did hurt," I say, shaking out my hand. "But it also felt good. Is that weird? I could do that entire freaking obstacle course right now."

"It's the adrenaline."

"No, I think it's finally having some justice."

His lips quirk. "Project Justice?"

"That's what I've named your contact in my phone."

He shakes his head. Only a short shake, one that shows he's still a little bemused by me. He looks at me as if I hung the moon. As if I'm some kind of goddess instead of just a rebel from nowhere. That means more to me than a million punches to Kyle's face.

Though that was fun, too.

"Head upstairs," Logan says gently.

"Aren't you coming with me?"

"Soon. I have a few more things to discuss with Kyle."

"I already hit him in the face. Are you saying that my punch was too weak?"

"Your punch was beautiful, Sunset. Let's just call these a few footnotes."

"I'm weirdly okay with that. I met your brother," I call out to Liam, who's been sitting back and watching this the entire time. "He said we're having dinner with his wife."

"I think you'll like her. She's a bestselling author."

"Oh my God. So you're with a world-class musician, and he's with a famous author?"

"My other brother, Josh, is married to a prima

ballerina."

"I see what you're doing there. Big, tough, military man with artsy girl."

Liam gives me a small smile of acknowledgment.

On the floor, Kyle groans.

I give Logan a quick kiss before turning to climb the metal stairs.

The air grows lighter, less oppressive, with each step.

Maybe it should be strange to trust someone who can be violent. Especially after my father. To me it makes perfect sense.

Oh, people like to think they're above it, but anyone can be violent.

A mother protecting her child, for example.

A man taking out his frustrations on his wife.

It's a certain kind of man who saves his violence for the people who truly deserve it, who protects not only his lover but even strangers. Who builds a large, welcoming family out of nothing but a few red flags.

CHAPTER TWENTY-TWO

W E SPEND THE next week with Liam and the rest of his family.

His brother Elijah is more rugged but also somehow more approachable. His wife is kind of quirky in a way that had me one-clicking her books before the night was over.

Most evenings we spend long hours at the dinner table, after the food and desserts have been put away, sharing outrageous stories over bottles of wine.

One night the boys go out for "HALO" which I assume is a video game until I realize they mean high-altitude military parachuting. The security dudes claim it's for training purposes, but I call bullshit, especially when Logan and Wolfgang tag along.

Worry eats at me. What's the point of getting

out of jail if you're going to jump out of planes? So, I invite Maisie over for a girls' night. She brings a card game called Romance vs The World, which turns out to be an effective distraction.

We laugh until we have tears in our eyes.

The guys get back early, having finished their jumps.

And clearly missing their women. Liam immediately disappears with Samantha. Everyone else soon breaks up. Wolfgang offers to take Maisie home, where she's still staying until we're ready to leave town.

Logan spends the night showing me the benefit to having a fearless, adrenaline junkie for a lover. He's full of sap, as they say around these parts, rowdy and mischievous, bending me over the bed, making me sit on his face, forcing me to orgasm so many times I collapse into a deep sleep.

The days pass in a beautiful dream.

Then it's time for us to travel to the next stop.

Cat approaches us just as we're about to board the RV. Her excitement radiates off her, making her dark eyes shine. It's a rare look for the usually combative Cat, one that instantly grabs my attention.

"Hey!" she says, her voice full of nervous energy.

I pause and turn to face her, a smile tugging at my lips despite my nervousness at whatever this is about. "What's up, Cat?"

She takes a deep breath, visibly gathering her courage. "I've decided to leave the circus," she blurts out, words rushing together in a torrent. "I'm going to college."

Holy shit. The revelation is both unexpected and somehow refreshing. Cat has always seemed so fiercely loyal to the circus, and this sudden shift is surprising.

Logan raises an eyebrow. "Does your mother know about this?"

Cat rolls her eyes, looking a little more like herself. "Yes, I talked to her in jail."

"It's a farm in Nebraska."

I make a face at Logan. "Are you still talking about that? It still sounds like you're trying to lie to the kids about what happened to old Roofus."

"It's a real place," he says.

"She can't leave," Cat points out. "That makes it jail."

"Considering I've just been from an actual jail, I assure you it's a farm."

Cat looks embarrassed, which sucks, but mostly I'm so grateful to hear the dry humor in Logan's tone. That's part of him just as much as his generosity and sensuality.

"I'm sorry," she says, her voice steadier now. "All my life I've followed in my mother's footsteps, did what she wanted. And regardless of whether she's at the farm or in the circus, I'm ready to be my own person. This is something I want for myself."

She looks between Logan and me, eyes wide, clearly anxious about our reactions.

He's quiet long enough to make my heart skip a beat.

"You were an incredible Juliet," I tell her. "But you should do what makes you happy. Besides, if everyone runs away to the circus, who's going to go to college anymore."

She grins. "My understudy is fabulous, as you know."

I snort, because I'm the understudy. But only because we didn't have time to train another person on all the moves. Since I helped choreograph them, I could do them in a pinch. "Thank you, but hopefully we can find someone else to do it. Besides, someone has to keep Tricks from eating all the treats when he's not onstage."

He wags his tail, looking up, clearly aware that something interesting is happening.

"You should do what makes you happy. We

should all have that freedom."

Her shoulders relax slightly at my words, relief washing over her features. "Thank you." She turns to look at Logan. "What do you think?"

Logan nods, his serious demeanor stern. "You have my support," he says.

Which is an interesting way to say it. Kind of old-fashioned. It might be quaint if it weren't for the stiff tone he's using.

Cat blinks her eyes as if fighting off tears.

"You're happy for her, right?" I ask, giving Logan a nudge behind his back.

He glances back. Those green eyes meet mine, the emerald gorgeous. And vivid. The kind of vivid that means he's emotional. And I realize that this sternness is coming from a different place. Not one of disapproval but grief.

"You'll miss her," I tell him, my voice soft but loud enough for her to hear.

"Of course I will." He turns back to her. "Cat, you were still a little kid when I came on. Now you're leaving. It's a big turning point. An important one. I'll miss you, but I would never want that to stop you from going."

Her eyes blink, and then her dark lashes glisten with tears. "Thank you," she whispers, emotion thickening her voice. "I appreciate everything. You were always... I could never... One day I hope..."

His voice comes out gruff. "No matter where life takes you, you'll always have a place in the Cirque des Miroirs."

She leans forward and gives him a hard squeeze around the middle. He freezes for a moment, hands in midair, before placing them around her shoulders.

She gives Logan some details, including a plan to attend a music program and to stay with an aunt in Florida until she gets in. He gives her a hug and promises to check in with her. Because sometimes love is taking someone with you. And sometimes it's letting someone go.

A shadow passing over his features. He crosses his arms, leaning against the RV, his gaze distant for a moment. I reach out and squeeze Logan's hand briefly before letting go.

Logan turns and follows me up the metal steps into the RV. Inside the cozy space that has been our sanctuary on the road, he sinks heavily onto the leather couch. I curl up beside him, resting my head on his broad shoulder.

Logan nods, staring into a space filled with memories. "It's bittersweet, isn't it? One chapter ends, another begins. Cat's growth... her independence… It's what I wanted for her, but it's strange for her to leave. Even Alessandra not being here is strange."

I gently squeeze his hand. "Does it feel like the circus is coming apart?"

He glances back. "No. It's strange but not in a bad way. It feels like we're just making room. For whoever needs to hitch a ride at the next town."

"That's right," he says, kissing my temple. "I've never thought much about the future before. There was only the next city, the next stop. Even next season seemed too long away to plan for. Now there's so much to look forward to."

"We might have a long time in the future," I state. "But even so. Let's not waste tonight," I reply, my voice a low silk thread in the dimness of the RV. His eyes—dark and fathomless—trace the contours of my face as if committing every line to memory.

"Sunset," he murmurs, a word that speaks volumes of the history we share, the scars we've earned, and the quiet understanding that has grown between us.

"Come with me." I take his hand, leading him through the narrow corridor. My fingers tangle with his, the calluses of his palm speaking of labor, of dedication, of love—for the circus, for the performers, for me.

His lips find mine, his kiss electric with connection, with desire. It's acknowledgment and need, a rawness that's a sharp juxtaposition to the circus pageantry. Clothes become whispers falling away. Skin meets skin with the urgency of a storm breaking over the big top. His hands trace the lines of my body, reading the story written there—old bruises, old scars, old pain. New passion. A whole new life.

His hands slip between my legs, where I'm already wet for him.

"Yes," I gasp, arching into him, feeling the raw power of his own need as he claims my lips again, deeper, possessive, as if he could rewrite my history with every touch, every kiss, erasing the chapters of pain and replacing them with verses of passion.

"Now," he breathes against my neck, sending shivers down my spine that cascade into waves of heat pooling within me. Our movements are a dance of shadows and whispers, a ballet choreographed by instinct and longing.

Here, in the embrace of the man who helped me escape the tightrope walk of my past, I find my footing. Here, only two miles away from my childhood home, I let go of my fears, surrendering to the safety of his arms, the belonging I feel nestled against his heart.

We move together, a symphony of sighs and murmurs, our bodies telling stories of resilience and rebirth, of a shared life woven from the magic and the mundane of our circus—a refuge where even the most battered souls can find sanctuary, can transform, can soar.

And as we crest and tumble, as the world outside fades into irrelevance, I understand that this is our reality—gritty and beautiful, full of risks and rewards. In Logan's embrace, under the canvas sky of our making, I am home.

CHAPTER TWENTY-THREE

STANDING AT THE entrance of the Passion Plunge roller coaster, adrenaline rushes through my veins. I'm not taking this journey alone. Logan's presence beside me, solid and reassuring, heightens the anticipation coiling in my chest. Our bodies press close together, the proximity electric, charged with a mix of excitement and something deeper, more primal.

Lust, perhaps.

He catches my eye, and my heart its own little upside down coaster. His hand slips into mine, warm and strong, and he gives it a gentle squeeze. "Ready?" he asks.

"Always," I say, breathless with both anticipation and desire.

"Should we sit in the front?" he asks.

"The back's faster."

"That's what they say. Let's find out."

We're the first people to ride. Ever.

There are other people riding—members of the circus, locals visiting the carnival. They're a blur as cross the loading area. My focus narrows to his hand in mine, the way his thumb traces small circles on my skin.

He releases my hand briefly to guide me into one of the seats, his touch lingering on my lower back. I slide into the seat, feeling the cool plastic against my thighs. Logan settles beside me. The safety bar lowers over our laps with a click.

A crooked smile playing on his lips. "Last chance to back out."

"Not a chance."

The ride operator's voice comes over the loud-speaker.

"Welcome to Passion Plunge, where love is the ultimate risk! Please move forward and find your seat. Pull the bar down until it clicks, because because this ride will sweep you off your feet—literally! Keep your hands and feet inside the car at all times."

A little buzzer goes off, and then we're off.

My heart pounds harder as we begin to as-cend.

His hand finds mine, threading our fingers

together. The anticipation builds with every second that passes. We climb higher and higher. The world around us falls away until it's just him and me, suspended between earth and sky.

We reach the crest of the hill, and for a brief moment, time seems to stand still.

I glance at his handsome profile…only to find he's already looking at me. His green eyes fill with a mixture of challenge and affection that takes my breath away.

The roller coaster moves inexorably forward. Anticipation coils tight inside me as we start the slow ascent to the top of the first drop. Each clank counts down to something terrifying. I grip Logan's hand tighter, and he responds with a firm squeeze.

As we inch close to the peak, the world below us shrinks. The rolling hills become a patchwork quilt of rooftops and streets, familiar yet distant. Up here, anything is possible. Like we're untethered from all the things that tried to hold us down.

Logan leans in closer, his breath warm against my ear. "You're mine now," he murmurs, a hint of a challenge in his voice. "The greatest ride of all."

I try to hide a smile. And fail. "Oh, I wouldn't

be sure about that. This one promises to be pretty good."

"I'm sure." His eyes are dark, intense, and filled with an unspoken promise. It's like he can see right through my tough exterior, straight into the parts of me that still get scared, that still feel vulnerable. And he loves every inch of me.

We reach the summit. The roller coaster pauses for a split second as if savoring our anticipation before plunging us into freefall. My stomach lurches, but instead of fear, I feel an exhilarating rush—like every cell in my body is alive and buzzing.

Then gravity takes over, pulling us into a wild descent that steals my breath and sends a thrill coursing through every nerve in my body. The world becomes a blur of colors and sensations, all blending into one heady experience. For these few moments, nothing else matters.

It's just us against gravity.

We twist and turn through loops and curves, our bodies pressed close together by the forces pulling us in every direction. Each time we catch our breath on a brief ascent before another wild descent, our eyes meet again—a silent reaffirmation of our connection.

We reach another peak. The momentum

doesn't even let us slow.

The coaster plummets down the second drop, and I let out a mixture of a scream and a laugh. The wind whips through my hair, making it fly around my face in wild strands. The thrill is electric, every nerve in my body tingling with exhilaration.

Logan's deep laughter resonates, a sound that grounds me even as we hurtle through the air. My heart races, but it's not just from the speed—it's from the feeling of being so alive, so free. The coaster curves hard, pressing me into Logan's hard body. His eyes flicker with excitement. And unmistakable lust, even this high off the ground. It's contagious. My body heats, especially when the coaster does the sudden slow down on another set off chains, taking us up to the last big drop. It feels hot after such an onslaught of cold wind. My cheeks still sting.

"Is this wild enough for you?"

"Yes," I say, breathless. "More than enough."

His lips quirk. "Oh, I wouldn't be sure about that. This one promises to be pretty good."

My eyes widen as he puts a hand on my thigh.

His fingers slip under the hem of my skirt. I suck in a breath as he slips beneath the fabric, his touch hot against my inner thigh. The roller coaster jolts, and I grip the safety bar with one hand, the other clutching his arm.

"Logan," I gasp, but his name is stolen by the wind whipping around us. His fingers trace higher, igniting a trail of fire on my skin. Each jolt and dip of the coaster amplifies the sensation, sending jolts of pleasure coursing through me.

His eyes lock on to mine, intense and full of hunger. He leans in, his lips brushing my ear. "Let go, Sienna." His voice is a low growl, barely audible over the clatter of the tracks.

And then we're diving into the final drop, this one even steeper than the last, and my stomach drops with it. Logan's touch anchors me, his fingers finding the sensitive spot between my legs. I arch into his hand, a moan escaping my lips. The sound is lost in the chaos of the ride, blending with the symphony of laughter and shrieks around us.

Logan's fingers move expertly, knowing exactly how to touch me, how to drive me wild.

I cling to him, my nails digging into his arm. The world around us blurs into a kaleidoscope of colors and sounds. The wind, the screams, the clatter of the tracks—it all fades away until it's just him and me, our bodies moving in sync with the roller coaster.

His breath hitches, and I know he's as affected as I am. The ride jostles us, throwing us against each other, our bodies pressing together in a dance of desire and danger. His touch grows more insistent, pushing me higher, closer to the precipice.

"Logan," I moan again, my voice barely a whisper against the roar of the ride. His name is a plea, a prayer, a promise.

We hit a series of rapid-fire curves, our bodies pushed from side to side by the G-forces. He lets the movement slide my body against his hand, allowing the coaster to do the work of making me aroused and hot, of driving me inexorably to climax. presence beside me makes everything sharper, more vivid.

On the final plunge, a deep curving swoop that takes us back toward the starting position, he pinches. And I come with a shuddering, gasping, needy orgasm. It goes on and on—even as the flash blinds me, my pleasure immortalized in an on-ride camera.

My body convulses, waves of ecstasy rippling through me. I cry out, the sound lost in the wind and the screams of the crowd. It's eaten by the snapping air, that sound.

No one knows. They're all screaming, throwing their hands in the air, even as Logan's hand rubs the hard, sensitive peak between my legs through the loops and spirals. The world spins around us in a blur of color and motion. Each twist and turn shedding another layer of the past—of Forrester, of all the things that tried to hold us down.

Just pure, unadulterated freedom.

His hand slips from beneath my skirt, but the heat of his touch lingers, a brand on my skin. I lean into him, my heart pounding in time with his. The ride comes to a halt, and for a moment, we just sit there, our bodies still pressed together, our breaths mingling.

The ride slows as we pull into the loading bay, the wild rush of wind easing into a gentle breeze. It's shaking. The ride is vibrating, broken. No, it's me that's shaking, overwhelmed by the exhilaration that defines this ride—our ride.

I turn to Logan, my breath still ragged from the ride and from him. His eyes meet mine, dark and intense, and without another thought, I press my lips to his.

Our kiss is fierce, fueled by adrenaline and desire. My fingers tangle in his hair, pulling him closer as the world around us fades into nothingness. His lips move against mine with a desperate urgency, our bodies still rocking with the rhythm of the ride.

He pulls back just enough to catch his breath, his eyes burning into mine. Then he licks his fingers slowly, savoring the taste of me. It sends a shiver down my spine, my body still thrumming with the aftershocks of pleasure.

I glance down at the bulge straining against his jeans and arch an eyebrow. "Do you want to go again?" I ask, my voice husky.

He meets my gaze with a look that sends a shiver down my spine—one filled with tenderness and something deeper... love. "Not here," he replies, echoing his words from that unforgettable night in jail. He leans in close, his breath hot against my ear. "The next time I come it's going to be inside you."

The promise in his words sends another wave of heat through me.

His fingers brush against mine, a silent acknowledgment of what we just shared. The connection between us is electric, and it's hard to pull away from it. The noise of the amusement park around us seems distant, almost unreal, compared to the intensity of this moment.

"Lovebirds, it's time to depart! Please unfasten your seatbelts and exit to the left. We hope your hearts are still racing. Thank you for riding, and don't forget to purchase you photos and Passion Plunge merch on your way out.

Time to disembark. We unbuckle ourselves and stand up. My legs wobble, but Logan steadies me with a hand on my waist.

As we step off the coaster platform onto solid ground, I can't help but steal another glance at him. There's something about the way he looks at me right now—like I'm the only person in the world—that makes me believe everything will be okay.

We walk away from the ride hand in hand, leaving behind the rush of adrenaline but carrying forward something even more exhilarating: each other. The ride's intensity mirrored the highs and lows we've faced together—the struggles, the passion, the moments of doubt followed by triumphs. Whatever comes next, we'll face it together.

Echoes of our passion pulse through my veins.

The night air cools my flushed skin.

Logan squeezes my hand, drawing me out of my thoughts. "You okay?" His voice is low, laced with concern and something deeper. "The ride wasn't too much?"

I give him a small smile. "It was too much. In

the best way."

The corner of his lips curves up. "It's been a hell of a ride, hasn't it?"

I can't help but grin. "You could say that."

As we leave the ride, I see the flickering lights of our tents and hear the distant murmur of voices—our family, our community. The performers who have become more than just colleagues; they've become part of our story.

We walk past the fortune teller's tent where Maisie is taking a video of herself. She catches sight of us and waves, her eyes twinkling with curiosity and excitement.

I give her a nod, feeling a swell of pride for how far we've come.

Logan pauses for a moment, turning to face me fully. His eyes search mine, as if looking for something he's afraid he might not find.

"Sienna," he starts, his voice serious but gentle. "I know things have been tough… for both of us. But I want you to know that no matter what happens next, I'm here. With you."

His words hit me hard, a lump forming in my throat. I squeeze his hand tighter, trying to convey everything I feel in that simple gesture.

"I know," I whisper back. "And I'm here with you too."

We continue walking, our steps synchronized as if we've been doing this dance forever. The lights from the big top glow in the distance, casting long shadows across the ground. It's a beacon calling us home.

The night is alive with possibilities, each moment brimming with unspoken promises and shared dreams. And as we stand hand in hand, I know that whatever comes next, we'll face it together—forever.

EPILOGUE

Logan

I STAND IN the center of the massive new big top, surveying the organized chaos around me. Workers scurry about, hoisting support beams and unfurling swaths of vibrant fabric. The new tent is a testament to our growth, to the even larger success of Cirque des Miroirs.

A sudden hush falls over the workers. I turn, following their uneasy gazes, and there he is. Emerson Durand, looking as polished and unruffled as ever in his tailored suit.

"Well, well," I drawl, raising an eyebrow. "Didn't expect to see you darken our doorstep again."

Emerson flashes that infuriatingly charming smile. "I'm ready to work, boss."

"Boss, is it?" I can't keep the wry amusement from my voice. "Must've gotten the wrong impression when you bailed on us in our hour of need."

A flicker of something—regret, maybe?—passes through Emerson's dark eyes, but it's gone in an instant. "Come now, Logan. I never signed up to follow some small-town girl's little ideas."

"Then you're in luck," I say, my tone hardening. "Because you won't be coming back to Cirque des Miroirs. Sienna's our creative director now."

Surprise registers on Emerson's face. "Logan, surely you can't be serious. Are you that pussy-whipped that you'll hand her your entire life's work?"

A rough laugh. "Emerson, if Sienna ever leaves me, she might as well take the circus with her. I'd be useless without her anyway." I step closer, my voice low. "But it doesn't matter. Not for you. You're not welcome here, period. Now leave."

Emerson's jaw clenches, anger flashing in his eyes. Along with what looks like pain. Though that can't be right. He doesn't feel emotions like the rest of us. For a moment, I think he might argue. But then he turns on his heel, striding away without another word.

I watch as he disappears into the sunset, the brilliant oranges and purples seeming to swallow him whole.

A pang of grief echoes in my chest.

The truth is that I miss him. There's no better ringmaster, though the circus is certainly not struggling. The real loss to me was someone I considered a great friend. He was loyal… until he wasn't.

And that doesn't work here.

The circus is about loyalty. About family.

About love, when it comes right down to it.

I see Sienna approaching from across the lot, her figure backlit by the golden light of the setting sun. There's something ethereal about her in moments like this, a fierce beauty that captivates everyone around her. I feel a smile tugging at my lips despite the tension coiled in my chest.

"Hey," she says, her voice tinged with concern. "I heard Emerson swung by."

The circus is also about gossip, I think wryly. News travels fast here.

"Came sniffing around for his job," I say, keeping my tone even.

"And?" Her eyes search mine, worry etched in their depths.

"I said no."

We lost one of the best ringmasters in the business, along with a top aerialist, but ticket sales are stronger than ever. Which is why we needed a bigger tent. And it's because of Sienna.

So, no, it's not because I'm pussy-whipped. Not because I want to spend every minute of every day with her. Though I am and I do. It's because she created a new beginning for the circus. And for me. She designed it.

The title of creative director belongs with her.

She looks troubled. "We could have used him."

"Absolutely not." I shake my head firmly. Emerson's betrayal cut deep; it's not something I'm willing to forgive so easily.

Her dark eyes fill with worry, making my heart clench. God, she's beautiful, especially in this glowing light. I take a moment to admire her strong features—bold like her but also sensitive and emotive.

"I love you so damn much," I say, my voice softening as I reach out to touch her cheek. "And I know the real reason you'd let him come back."

"Because you care about him," she says softly.

"I care about *you*," I say, gently but firmly. The thought of anyone disrespecting Sienna and staying in this circus is unthinkable.

She looks like she's going to argue, her eyes narrowing slightly in that determined way of hers. It's sweet, but it's also not going to happen.

Before she can get a word out, I pull her close and kiss her deeply. Her lips are warm and soft against mine, and for a moment, all the worries and uncertainties fade away.

Tricks runs up and jumps on our legs, wanting to be part of the embrace. Laughing, I bend down and pick him up, holding him to my chest as Sienna gives him baby talk. "You want kisses too, don't you?" she coos, and the little guy pants happily at her. *I know the feeling, buddy.*

I put the dog back down and tell Sienna, "Get going, but come back in a couple hours. When the tent is back up." I pause, a smirk playing on my lips. "After all… we have to break it in."

Her eyes widen, a flush creeping up her cheeks. "How?" she asks, her voice barely above a whisper.

Leaning in, I murmur something filthy and specific in her ear, detailing exactly what I'm going to do to her delicious body to christen the new tent. It involves licking her pussy until she comes. Then I'm going to test the frame of the new acrobatics assembly by fucking her in one of the swings.

Her breath hitches, and I can see the pulse in her neck quicken. She swallows hard, her dark eyes meeting mine with a mix of anticipation and desire. I'm also looking forward to testing out the new acoustics with her moans and whimpers.

I step back, giving her a playful wink. "See you soon, Sunset."

She nods, a small smile playing on her lips as she turns to leave. I watch her go, the sway of her hips holding my gaze until she disappears into the bustling clamor of a circus setup.

Tricks trots after her, tail wagging.

Yeah, we're both goners over this girl. And we wouldn't have it any other way.

✧　✧　✧

What will Emerson do to earn his way back into the circus?

Is the "farm" a real place?

Find out in BLUE MOON, available now!

Charismatic. Devious. Secretive. Emerson Durand is the ringmaster for the illustrious Cirque des Miroirs. In each city he finds a new woman to command for the night. Until he finds the one woman who doesn't bow to his demands.

Luna Rider soars through the air as an aerial acrobat. She's determined to provide for herself and her sister, but she doesn't count on being gambled away. Or the secrets that hover under the striped tent.

Get BLUE MOON now!

And you can read the story of ex-military Liam North who ends up the guardian of violin prodigy Samantha, only a few hours away from the town of Forrester.

Get OVERTURE now!

Turn the page for an excerpt from OVERTURE.

✦ ✦ ✦

S OMETHING BECAME WARM inside me. Warm and new. Eighteen years old means I know what sex is about but I've never seen it, not that close, not with a man I looked up to like a father. Well, not exactly a father.

He might have had legal custody of me, but I've never quite seen him as a father.

Something flashes through Liam's dark eyes. Worry? "Is it the tour?"

"No, of course not. I'm ready for the tour." Though *ready* isn't exactly the word I would use to describe myself. Terrified and breathless, maybe. The interview also drove home how soon I'll leave for the tour. Three months from now I'll walk out these doors.

Three months from now everything will change.

Liam puts his hand on my forehead, the contact so sudden I make a squeak of surprise. "No fever," he mutters, more to himself than to me. "Should I call Dr. Foster?"

"It's probably nothing," I say quickly, besieged by an image of the doctor making a house call. *Wet,* he would announce after an examination. *And flushed. And clenching her thighs every time you look at her. It's an acute case of lust, I'm*

I can understand Liam's surprise. When's the last time I caught a cold?

Maybe never.

In this household bodies are treated like one of the well-oiled guns in his cabinet. Organic vegetables and grass-fed beef. We sleep on a schedule designed for optimum performance. There's no entry in the procedure for *Samantha has a crush on Liam North, the man who's taken care of her for the last six years.*

"Rest," he says, nodding his head, decisive. "You'll take the rest of the day off."

"I'm sure I'll feel better tomorrow." Maybe once I've hidden under the covers, touching myself and pretending it's him, making myself come about a thousand times.

His brows draw together. It's a strange look on him. It takes me a minute to place it— uncertainty. He's never looked uncertain before. "Maybe I *should* call the doctor."

"God. No. Please."

That only makes his expression more severe. "Samantha. Are you sure?"

He doesn't wait for an answer. Two fingers tilt my chin up. His other hand holds my face up for his focus. His thumb brushes my eyebrow. My cheek. My jaw. All entirely ordinary places on a body, somehow lit by a thousand lights. There's no reason a man can't touch a young woman he considers his daughter, when he's worried that she's sick. It doesn't mean he wants to have sex with her, never that.

Except he looks a little shaken when he's done with his perusal, his eyes blinking as if surprised to find himself touching me, his throat working as he swallows. "You would tell me if something were wrong."

Not a question. It's a statement. "Yes."

I manage not to add *sir*, but only barely.

When I first moved here, I called him *sir* like the young recruits he trained. *Yes, sir. No, sir.* He inspires that kind of respect. The people from his company would raise their eyebrows when they heard me say it. *You run a tight ship,* they would say, sounding impressed and a little intimidated.

He told me not to, but it still slips out when I'm nervous.

You're not under my command, he muttered in a rare show of impatience, even though it feels like I am. Who else would I be under?

He's the one who gives me orders. I'm the one who obeys. We both know who's in charge.

It's like he can hear the unspoken *sir* anyway.

His jaw tightens. "Go," he says.

He doesn't take a step back. Instead he watches while I bend to place my violin and bow in the case and close it. I stand up, but there's no room to stand or walk or breathe. He's filling every square inch of the room with his broad chest and dark eyes. Logically I know that I can walk around him, that he's waiting for me to do that, but somehow I'm standing here, one inch away from him, my small breasts almost brushing his chest when I breathe in and out.

There are foreign mercenaries and four-star generals who walk through these hallways. Large men. Muscled men, but none of them compare to Liam. There are a few sets of weights in the gym downstairs, but he doesn't use them. You practice the way you perform. That's what he taught me about the violin. It's the way he approaches his work, spending hours a day in the obstacle course that takes up a few acres in back.

Soldiers ten years younger than him can't keep up.

I know he's a large man, but it still feels impossible to look up far enough. When I meet his gaze, awareness sparks from him to me, every place on my body that's an inch away from his.

"Tomorrow," he says, his voice somehow

lower. "You'll be yourself again tomorrow."

God, I want that to be true. I'm not sure who that is anymore. The obedient girl who practices her violin for hours every afternoon? Not exactly. No matter how much he wants that to be true. Something is going to happen tonight.

I'm not sure whether I'll become more myself—or less.

Want to read more? Order OVERTURE now!

Books by Skye Warren

North Security Trilogy & more North brothers

Overture

Concerto

Sonata

Audition

Diamond in the Rough

Silver Lining

Gold Mine

Finale

Rochester Trilogy & more

Private Property

Strict Confidence

Best Kept Secret

Hiding Places

Behind Closed Doors

Endgame Trilogy & more books in Tanglewood

The Pawn

The Knight

The Castle

The King

The Queen

Escort

Survival of the Richest
The Evolution of Man
Mating Theory
The Bishop

Chicago Underground series
Rough
Hard
Fierce
Wild
Dirty
Secret
Sweet
Deep

Stripped series
Tough Love
Love the Way You Lie
Better When It Hurts
Even Better
Pretty When You Cry
Caught for Christmas
Hold You Against Me
To the Ends of the Earth

The Modern Fairy Tale Duet

Beauty and the Professor

Falling for the Beast

For a complete listing of Skye Warren books, visit

www.skyewarren.com/books

About the Author

Skye Warren is the bestselling author of dangerous romance such as the Endgame trilogy. Her books have been on the New York Times, the USA Today, and the Wall Street Journal bestseller lists. They feature powerful men and the strong women who bring them to their knees. She makes her home in Texas with her loving family, sweet dogs, and flying squirrel.

Sign up for Skye's newsletter:
skyewarren.com/newsletter

Like Skye Warren on Facebook:
facebook.com/skyewarren

Join Skye Warren's Dark Room reader group:
skyewarren.com/darkroom

Follow Skye Warren on Instagram:
instagram.com/skyewarrenbooks

Visit Skye's website for her current booklist:
skyewarren.com/books

Copyright

This is a work of fiction. Any resemblance to actual persons, living or dead, business establishments, events or locales is entirely coincidental. All rights reserved. Except for use in a review, the reproduction or use of this work in any part is forbidden without the express written permission of the author.

Black Sheep © 2024 by Skye Warren
Print Edition

Formatting by BB eBooks
Cover by Book Beautiful
Proofreading by Sisters Get Lit.erary